Was it a mistake? Meredith touched the patch of stubby hair behind her ear again and her fingers froze.

It was no mistake. The shorn area near her scalp was about the size of a half dollar, and the short hairs were blunt where they had been cut.

In her mind she heard the sharp snip of scissors and recognized it as the sound that had awakened her from her dream. The misty landscape was clearing, and she was beginning to remember it all, even the words that had been whispered with her name. The room began to spin and a terrible black fear enveloped her. A scream rose in her throat as the words she'd been unable to recall on waking now burned themselves into her consciousness forever.

MEREDITH, MEREDITH. YOU ARE IN MY POWER.

LAUREL-LEAF BOOKS

The Power

BETSY HAYNES

TWILIGHT™

WHERE DARKNESS BEGINS...

Published by
Dell Publishing Co., Inc.
1 Dag Hammarskjold Plaza
New York, N.Y. 10017

Laurel-Leaf Library ® TM 766734,
Dell Publishing Co., Inc.

Twilight™ is a trademark of Dell Publishing Co., Inc.,
New York, New York.

ISBN: 0-440-97164-0

RL: 6.6

Printed in the United States of America

First printing—October 1982
Second printing—January 1983

Book Club Edition

Chapter One

Will this storm ever let up? Meredith Turner looked up at her rain-splattered window into the inky night sky and sighed dispiritedly. A clap of thunder at that moment punctuated her feeling of gloom. Meredith couldn't remember a thunderstorm ever in October in this part of western Massachusetts. But in a way she felt it was appropriate; it was as if the sky were sympathizing with her depression.

She felt even the lightning, an unusual series of bright red flashes that lit up the sky, was put up there for her alone.

Turning her head, Meredith pointed her gaze to her left ring finger, bare now that Kit had asked for his class ring back after a sudden fight that morning. Uncontrollably, tears began to well up in her eyes, and she realized how lost she felt without him. "Oh Kit," she sobbed. "Why did you have to leave me now when I need you so much?"

Meredith allowed herself to give in to the loss for a moment, then tried to pull herself together to finish the work that had to be done. Sighing heavily, she picked up a red marker and returned her attention to the campaign poster spread across her desk. It read: MEREDITH TURNER FOR JUNIOR STUDENT COUNCIL REP. Or at least it would say that when she finished the sign, which along with the others piled neatly on her floor would go up on the school walls in the morning. *If* she ever finished it. With a start she looked at the digital alarm clock on her desk: 9:48. She didn't have much time. Pressing harder than she should, she colored in the *M*. The marker seeped across the pencil outlines, through the paper, and onto her desk, like a gaping blood wound that wouldn't clot.

She stared at the ugly thing and sank

further into depression. Tomorrow she had to make a campaign speech before the all-school assembly, and she still had work to do on that before calling it a night. But where she was going to find the words she didn't know. She always got flustered when she had to speak in front of a group. Her stomach tightened as she recalled how she'd blundered through an oral report for her history class just last month. She'd frozen as soon as she looked out at the sea of her classmates' faces. Stuttering, she'd raced through her presentation, completely forgetting the carefully prepared notes in front of her. If only she could send someone up there in her place tomorrow.

Just thinking about it made her drop the marker on the desk in dismay. "Kit Van Leer, this is all your fault," she whispered under her breath, quiet enough so her parents in their next-door bedroom couldn't hear. "If you hadn't talked me into running for this stupid office, I wouldn't be going through this anxiety right now!"

Until this morning it had made perfect sense to Meredith for her to run with Kit for the two junior-class seats. They had been inseparable almost from the first day they met in ninth grade, and everyone at Denniston considered them a wonderful-looking couple: Kit—tall with gorgeous blue eyes, wheat-colored hair, and classic Dutch looks — and Meredith — also tall, with long blond hair and aquamarine eyes that set off her milk-white skin. Everyone always told her how much she and Kit seemed to belong together, as if they had been picked by Destiny to be united. She had never doubted that and thought Kit hadn't either, until what had begun as a simple little request this morning exploded into a near-shouting match that ended with him asking for his ring back.

To Meredith it had seemed innocent enough — a request for help on that dreaded speech. She was surprised when he turned her down, saying it wouldn't be right for one candidate to help another; after all, they did everything else together, why not this? But Kit was firm on the point, maintaining that to help her write her speech would be morally wrong and unfair to the other two candidates. The more she objected, the more he stood his ground. Tears burned in Meredith's eyes as she remembered the awful scene. "How could he let me down like this?" she moaned.

The sky continued to light up menacingly, and the lamp on her desk flickered momentarily as Meredith tried to concentrate on the task before her. When the light returned to full strength Meredith nervously continued coloring in the big block letters. The rain seemed to be coming down harder now, and after she'd raced through the word COUNCIL, Meredith flipped on her radio to see if she could find a weather report. The last thing she needed, she told herself, was a set of rain-soaked, illegible posters. She wanted to be prepared.

The weather was playing havoc with the reception, creating static on the Springfield rock station she usually listened to. She slowly turned the dial to find the local station in Denniston, passing by an announcer introducing a big-band song, and a radio evangelist raging about eternal damnation, before coming to rest on the last bars of a stringed instrumental she couldn't quite place.

The soothing beautiful music seemed to calm her down a bit as she colored in the last word on the poster. Her worrying had exhausted her and she hoped the announcer would break in before she was lulled to sleep by the music. She rubbed her eyes and raked her hands through her blond hair in an effort to stay awake.

As Meredith was filling in the *P* in REP, a man with a sonorous voice came on with the ten o'clock news. She was only half listening until the announcer said, "Massachusetts state police are still on the lookout for George Sondergard, who escaped this afternoon from the Springfield State Hospital. The thirty-five-year-old Sondergard had been under observation following his conviction last week in a series of drowning deaths in Pittsfield. Police believe he is armed and dangerous and headed in the vicinity of Hadley. If anyone has seen . . ."

An involuntary shudder went through Meredith as she heard the report. Hadley was the next town over from Denniston. The storm must be making me jumpier than usual, she tried to convince herself as she put the finishing touches on the poster. Still, she kept thinking about the report. She was so preoccupied with thoughts of the escapee that she forgot the weather report.

With the radio on in the background Meredith changed into her nightgown, telling herself she'd do a better job on her speech after she'd gotten some sleep. She felt safer under the covers, although the house was certainly secure enough. After a series of robberies in the neighborhood the year before, her father had placed new locks on all the windows and doors. As she pulled down the quilted coverlet and slipped between the light pink percale sheets, she found the music was once again having a lulling effect on her. She decided to keep the radio on all night.

Meredith closed her eyes and wished for sleep to rescue her from her worries. But phrases from the radio report kept running through her head until at last exhaustion from the draining day overtook her and she fell into a deep sleep. . . .

Suddenly Meredith awoke and opened her eyes. She was drenched in a cold sweat and her heart pounded against her chest until she thought it would break through her ribs.

She thought she'd heard something. Had someone called her name? As she gasped to regain her breath Meredith tried to remember what had awakened her. There had been a sharp sound, something wicked that had pierced her heart. What was it?

Again she heard something and sat bolt upright, hitting her head on the brass headboard. She tried to look for the source of the sound, but the darkness was so complete she couldn't even see the fingers she raised in front of her face. The only light came from the digital clock. Squinting, Meredith made out the narrow red numbers: 4:38.

Straining her ears, she listened for the sound and heard a soft thump. Was that it? Meredith caught her breath in terror. Then she realized it was only Mr. McGinty delivering the morning papers. "I must have been dreaming," she told herself, trying to slow her heartbeat. "I'm so keyed up. The sound of Mr. McGinty's footsteps must have triggered something in a dream."

Meredith shivered and became aware of a coolness in the room. Fearfully she got out of bed and tiptoed to the window. It was open. Meredith felt sure she'd closed it when the storm began, but now in her jittery state she wasn't positive.

She stared out into the blankness of the night and shivered again. Gradually the eastern sky was lightening. The rain had stopped and in its place was a dense fog that obscured the normally scenic view. Suddenly she remembered. There had been fog in her dream too.

She had to get a grip on the fragments of the dream that raced through her head. "Yes," she breathed as she remembered she had been walking along a cobblestone path. The feeling that she'd been there before gnawed at her and as she closed her eyes, trying to refocus the vision in her mind, she froze. She could see eyes the color of rubies burning at the end of the pathway. She found herself being drawn to the gaze, helped along by a swirling mist that brushed her cheeks like gentle fingertips.

She pulled back from her recollection in terror and tried to slow her racing heart. She thought again of the sound she'd heard. Had someone called her name? Was that the sound she'd heard? It was an urgent sound, she remembered, a voice that drew her along through the mist. She had hurried along the path, her footsteps echoing back to her and drowning out all other sounds — except that voice. That voice that so inexplicably attracted her.

At the end of the path was a blankness which, she saw as she drew near, was actually a murky bottomless pool. The voice beckoned her to enter and as she did so, she was slowly enveloped in the water's warmth. The water was comforting at first, but as she sank deeper and deeper, spinning as if in a whirlpool, she realized she was in a cold and uncomfortable place. She wanted to escape, but the voice commanded her to stay. Again and again she heard her name, and with it came other words whispered too softly for her to make them out.

Meredith leaned against the window frame feeling weak and breathless. "It was only a dream," she said aloud, hugging herself in the chilly night air. "At this rate I'll never get any sleep. I can't let it get to me."

Slowly Meredith tiptoed back to the

warmth of her bed. As she pulled the covers up to her ears, she whispered, "This is what I get for having that maniac on my mind." Trying to dismiss the disturbing vividness of her dream, she thought, I've got to get some rest or I'll never be able to give my speech tomorrow. I'll just listen to some more of that drowsy music.

But the radio was silent. Meredith didn't remember having turned it off and she felt her heart beat faster again. Then as she turned over onto her right side, the thought occurred to her that perhaps her mother had heard the music and come into her room. Yes, her mother could have turned off the radio and then opened the window to let in some fresh cool air. That would explain things.

Slowly Meredith felt her muscles relax and she dropped off to sleep again. Just before she awoke, she heard a sharp sound and felt something swoop toward her, aiming for her head, swirling around and around like a crazed bat. She opened her eyes to see what it was, but she could see only shadows. When she closed her eyes the sensation returned, and with it the prickling feeling of unidentified fear. Out of desperation she got up again and switched on her desk lamp. It was 5:32.

An hour and a half later Meredith was

downstairs in the kitchen breakfast nook, nursing a cup of hot chocolate she couldn't bring herself to drink.

"You were up early, weren't you?" her mother said, walking into the room.

"I wanted to work on my speech," Meredith said. "I couldn't sleep anyway."

"Nightmares?" her mother asked.

Meredith almost spilled the hot chocolate across the table. "As a matter of fact, yes," she told her mother. Shivering, she remembered the terror she'd felt, but strangely, she couldn't recall any of the specifics of the dream. "I heard about this escaped convict right before I went to bed."

"I heard about him too. At least it got Kit off your mind," her mother said in a futile attempt to cheer up her daughter. "You know better than to let something as silly as a dream get to you," she said breezily. "Your mind was just playing tricks on you."

"I hope you're right," Meredith answered, shrugging off the eerie memory.

"Besides, this is your special day," her mother went on. "Everything will be fine."

"You're such an optimist, Mother," Meredith muttered. "I mean, just look." She pointed to the rain, once again bathing the atmosphere like a slow-motion waterfall. "The one day I have to look good. My hair's going to be a frizzball by the time of the assembly. And the rain will probably ruin these posters."

"Take my word for it. You look beautiful. That blue sweater makes your eyes sparkle like sapphires."

"Thanks, Mother." Meredith blushed. "I suppose I'm making more out of it than I should." She gave her mother a weak smile.

"That's the spirit," her mother replied. "As far as the posters go, why don't you put plastic wrap around them, and I'll drive you to school on my way to work." She put down her cup of coffee. "Besides, I don't want that escaped lunatic Sondergard going after my daughter. I heard about him on the radio this morning."

"Do you really think he's coming to Denniston?" Meredith asked in trepidation.

Her mother laughed. "No, dear," she said. "The chances of that happening are slim. Don't be such a worrywart, okay? It's so unlike you."

"Oh, Mother." Meredith sighed. But she told herself her mother was right. She had nothing to worry about after all.

Chapter Two

It was raining harder by the time Meg Turner dropped Meredith off at Denniston High School. Now that Meredith had put the memory of the dreams behind her, she felt ready to turn her attention to the real problem facing her—how she would manage to get through this important day. Already one of her fears was materializing. She could almost feel her hair turning to frizz as she ran up the narrow marble steps to the old charcoal-colored building, hunched over her rolled up posters. Practically breathless, she opened the double front doors made of heavy lead glass and breathed a sigh of relief when she saw two of her best friends waiting there for her.

"Am I glad to see you," she said.

"It's about time you got here," Liz Elsberry said impatiently, taking the posters from Meredith's soaking arms. "What'd you do, oversleep?"

Meredith shot Liz a weak smile. Meredith had always admired Liz's straightforward manner, but the mention of sleep brought back thoughts of that dream, thoughts she didn't want to be reminded of.

"Don't mind her, Madam Student Councilperson," called Patti Hayden in a singsong voice as she bowed before her. "Your helpers await you."

"Thanks, Patti," said Meredith. "I appreciate it." Then looking at the ancient round-faced clock on the wall, she added, "Look, I'm only five minutes late. Where's Missy?"

"Late as usual," Liz muttered in reference to Missy Price, the fourth member of their group.

"It doesn't matter. We're still the first ones here," Patti added. "If we work fast, we can get your posters in all the best spots before the others show up."

"Then what are we waiting for?" said Meredith with renewed vigor. "Let's get going. Missy'll catch up with us later."

The three girls hurried up and down the halls, tacking posters to bulletin boards and taping them to walls. The plastic wrap Meredith had put around her posters kept them dry, and they survived the trip through the elements in perfect shape. Meredith was pleased, too, with the way they had turned out — with the exception of the poster with the drippy red *M*. It looked creepy, but there was nothing she could do about it now.

Meredith was truly grateful for her friends' help. Liz, Patti, and Missy were the best friends she could ask for. Liz Elsberry, who was the center on the girls' basketball team, was taller than Meredith by a couple of inches, and they'd been friends for years. Liz sometimes dated Curt Lockwood, one of Kit's friends from the track team, and they'd double-dated many times. At least they had before she and Kit broke up.

In contrast to Liz, Patti Hayden was barely five feet tall, a roly-poly who was always dieting. Her curly permed hair made her face look even rounder than it was, but her sunny disposition gave her an inner beauty that Meredith truly admired.

And then there was Missy. She was the same height as Meredith and they wore their hair in the same style. In fact sometimes they were mistaken for sisters. There was a special, almost sisterly understanding between them, too. With a pang Meredith wished Missy were here now. Missy would understand her nervousness about the election better than anyone.

Meredith's thoughts returned to the posters she had to hang. Gradually the three girls were joined by friends of the other three candidates who added their own colorful posters to the dingy, drab corridors of the school.

"I guess Missy's not coming," Meredith said after they finished tacking up a poster next to the administration offices.

"You know her, she probably just forgot," said Liz drily. "I swear, sometimes that girl lives in another world."

"Just because she cares about more things than football scores and the latest gossip does not make her 'out of this world,'" Meredith said in defense of her friend.

"I wonder if we'll run into Kit," said Patti in an attempt to change the subject.

"That worm," muttered Liz. "I can tell you what I'd do if I met up with him." Liz had been upset at the abrupt way Kit had treated Meredith and didn't mind letting anyone know how she felt.

"Come on, Liz," Meredith pleaded. "Maybe Kit and I will work things out."

Liz shot her a fierce look. "How can you want him back after the way he treated you yesterday? If I were you I'd look around these gray halls for some new blood. There's more than one cute boy in this school."

"And there are a lot of creepy ones, too," added Patti, wrinkling her nose.

Meredith was silent. Secretly she hoped she *would* meet Kit in the hallway. She wanted to see how he would look at her today, see if there would be any hint in his eyes that he still cared for her. She'd fallen in love with him because of his eyes, those deep blue eyes that filled with tenderness when he looked at her. She needed to know before they walked out on stage if there was a chance he'd ever feel that way again. She couldn't really believe he wanted to give up everything they had just because of one silly fight.

The first bell rang, and the three girls hurried up the stairs to the third-floor juniors' locker center. By this point the air was filled with the slamming of doors and the shouts and laughter of students getting ready for the school day.

Meredith stopped short as they approached the rows of old green lockers. She

17

thought she heard something sharp in her ears. Patti, noticing Meredith's pained expression, put her hand on her shoulder.

"Hey, what's wrong?"

"Huh? Oh, um, nothing. I just thought I heard something," Meredith said quietly. It sounded vaguely like the distorted voice she'd heard in her dream.

"Come on, we'll be late," scolded Liz. Glancing at Meredith's almost haunted expression, she added, "I saw you looking at his locker, Meredith Turner."

"I was not!"

Any further protestations from Liz were interrupted by Patti's shout. "Hey, look." She was pointing ahead. "What's that on your locker, Meredith?"

The three girls focused their attention on a small box which hung by a string from Meredith's big Yale lock. It was about the size of a cigarette pack and looked as if it had been cut down from a larger box.

"Ooh la la," teased Patti. "A secret admirer."

"Or a time bomb planted by one of your opponents," offered Liz with a wry grin.

Or maybe it's from Kit, thought Meredith to herself. She didn't want to tell the others she hoped it was his class ring. Maybe he wants me to have it back, but doesn't know how to say so. She sighed. That was always the way it was with Kit. In the three years she'd dated him she'd learned he was too shy to come right out and say what he really meant, especially when it came to expressing emotions like love. It'd be just like him to leave a little box with a funny message inside, something like: Dear Meredith: Forgive me. This ring looks much prettier on your hand than mine.

Meredith reached for the box and immediately discovered the fallacy in her thinking. From the lightness of the package it was clear there was no ring inside. She snapped the flimsy string off and pulled open the lid as Liz and Patti crept up behind her. Whatever was inside was still hidden by a folded piece of tissue that puffed up in the center.

"What is it?" whispered Patti, who was partially hidden from the box by her two tall friends.

"Open it," Liz said impatiently.

Meredith parted the tissue with a finger and then drew back in surprise. Again she thought she heard that hollow-sounding voice echo through her head. "It's a lock of hair," she said, dumbfounded.

The three girls stared at the golden curl resting on the tissue. "Why would anyone give me a lock of hair?" Meredith asked, shaking her head in disbelief. Gingerly she lifted the curl and held it in the air with two fingers — and almost dropped it in fright. She'd felt an inexplicable tingle of terror rise up her spine as she'd touched the hair. "How silly," she said aloud.

"Look!" cried Patti, peering into the box. Wide-eyed, she pointed to the bottom.

Scrawled there in blood-red letters were the words: YOU ARE IN MY POWER!

"That's ridiculous." Meredith shook her head uneasily. "I'm not in anyone's power." She dropped the lock of hair back into the box, covering the terrible message. But the words burned in her brain, and the same pricking fear she'd felt when she'd touched the hair crept up her spine again.

Liz began to reach for the blond curl. "Don't touch it!" Meredith shouted uncontrollably.

Liz drew her hand back. "What's the big deal?" she said, casting a quizzical look toward Meredith. "It looks like your hair to me. I just wanted to see if it matched."

"That's crazy," Meredith shot back. "It's just someone's stupid idea of a joke."

"Sure," said Patti. You must have an admirer with a weird sense of humor. Remember last year when somebody put a dead rat in Christie Nevell's gym locker? The same nut probably did this, too."

"On the other hand," Liz said, stroking

her chin thoughtfully, "this could be the work of that guy who ran out of the loony bin yesterday."

"Liz," Patti scoffed, "you don't really think some maniac—"

Liz held up her hands and laughed. "Only joking, girls."

"Yeah, we're making too much of this," Meredith said lightly. "It's just a practical joke."

"You know, Meredith, I think your little jokester just handed you a great slogan." Patti laughed and raised her hands as if she were about to pounce on her two friends. Rolling her eyes menacingly she hissed, "You must vote for me because YOU ARE IN MY POWER!"

Liz giggled and nodded her head in agreement. Meredith laughed too, but a disturbing thought began to enter her mind. No matter what anyone else thought, this was no joke. There was something sinister about the message in the box, something threatening about the lock of hair. Could there also be a connection between this "gift" and her dream? The thought chilled her.

"Are you all right, Meredith?" asked Patti. "You're not taking this seriously, are you?"

"Oh no," she lied. She had to think about this, to come up with a reasonable explanation for the strange message. The last thing she needed was for them to think she was a scared little baby, afraid of a silly, harmless joke.

"We'd better get moving or we're going to be late," said Liz in her most serious voice. "It's time for the second bell already. We'll talk more at lunch."

As Liz and Patti hurried off, Meredith dropped the box into her canvas bag and opened her locker to get her books for the day, catching sight of herself in the mirror hanging on the inside of the door. Patti was right—she looked terrible, like she'd been spooked or something. Closing her eyes she took a deep breath. She had to relax. She couldn't let this thing get to her, not with the big assembly just hours away. She just couldn't!

After stuffing her canvas bag into her locker and gathering her books, Meredith headed quickly to her first class. Rounding the last corner, she stopped at the sight of a black and gold poster hanging above the drinking fountain on the right side of the hall. VOTE FOR KIT VAN LEER, it said. The sight of Kit's name brought a lump to her throat, but she hurried on, pretending he didn't mean anything to her at all.

Madame Dussault was standing in her

usual spot outside the French III classroom door. The French teacher was a small woman who always wore black clothes to match her pitch-black hair — she looked as if she were in perpetual mourning. The rumor around school was that her lover had been killed the night before their wedding, the murderer never caught.

But today Meredith thought only of how normal it was to see Madame Dussault waiting to exchange greetings with her entering students as was the custom each day.

"Bonjour, Mademoiselle Turner. Ca va?"

"Bonjour, Madame Dussault," murmured Meredith, barely able to speak the words. *"Ca va bien, merci."*

Meredith slid into her seat and opened her French book to the assigned page. The classroom was filling with students but she kept her eyes turned downward. She didn't feel like conversing much today.

Usually she liked being in the French room with its posters of the Eiffel Tower and other Paris street scenes. Often she'd pretend she was there preparing for an extended trip abroad, where she'd dazzle at least half a dozen handsome Frenchmen with her flawless French. But today as the final bell rang and class began, she was oblivious to the international flavor of the room.

YOU ARE IN MY POWER. The words played over and over in her mind like some half-forgotten song. She had heard them before. She felt it. She was sure of it. But where? In some old Dracula movie? She caught herself gasping, was it in her dream? Were those the words uttered by the figure with the ruby-red eyes? Blood eyes, she thought. She shuddered at the memory and willed herself back to the droning voice of Madame Dussault.

"Today, *mes amis*, we will decline the French verb *couper*, to cut."

Cut. Snip. Lock of hair. Meredith immediately flashed on an image of scissors. She had seen them in her dream, she remembered now, a giant gleaming instrument wielded by a disembodied hand. That had been the strange thing hovering about her head. Could that lock of hair really be hers? She laughed nervously, trying to dismiss the thought. How could anyone have gotten close enough to snip a lock of her hair without her knowing it?

She slowly raised her hand and nervously twirled a strand of her hair. She wanted to make sure the lock of hair wasn't her own. A wild urgency overtook her. She had to be certain.

Madame Dussault was writing sentences on the blackboard, and most of the students were dutifully copying them down. But Meredith was oblivious to the events in the room. Only one thing mattered.

She raked her fingers outward from her scalp to the ends of her hair, starting on the right side of her head. Again and again she combed the strands, but nothing seemed to be missing. A sense of relief began to wash over her as she reached the back of her head. She was being foolish — it wasn't her hair in the box after all. Still she continued the search, shifting to her left hand, beginning at the scalp and working outward as before. It had to be a joke, she told herself over and over, and the joker was probably someone right here in her French class, watching her out of the corner of an eye and laughing as she searched in vain for that missing curl.

Meredith felt her face flush at the thought of being watched, and she started to withdraw her hand — just as her fingers found a patch of stubby hair behind her left ear. Was it a mistake? She touched the spot again and her fingers froze.

It was no mistake. The shorn area near her scalp was about the size of a half-dollar, and the short hairs were blunt where they had been cut.

In her mind she heard the sharp snip of scissors and recognized it as the sound that had awakened her from her second dream. The misty landscape from her first dream, too, was clearing, and she was beginning to remember it all, even the words that had been whispered with her name. The room began to spin and a terrible black fear enveloped her as the words she'd been unable to recall on waking now burned themselves into her consciousness forever.

MEREDITH. MEREDITH. YOU ARE IN MY POWER.

Chapter Three

"*Mademoiselle Turner? Qu'est-ce que vous avez?*"

The sound of Madame Dussault's voice penetrated the curtain of fear surrounding Meredith's mind, but at first she couldn't comprehend the words.

"Can you hear me, Meredith? What's wrong?"

The small Frenchwoman shook her pupil lightly and Meredith began to realize where she was. She looked around and saw the classroom was empty except for the two of them. What had happened? Where had everyone gone?

"Meredith, what is it? You're pale. Did something frighten you?" Her eyes wide with concern, Madame Dussault stared at her student.

"I—" Meredith tried to explain, but she wasn't sure herself what had happened. She must have blacked out. "I don't know what came over me," she said weakly.

Students for the next period's class began filtering into the room. The pale-faced girl gave her teacher a half-smile. "I guess I'd better get to my next class before the bell rings."

"But are you certain you're all right? You can sit here and rest a bit if you wish."

Meredith realized the entering students were staring at her. She wanted to be alone so she could figure out what had happened. Rising from her seat she said, "Thank you, but I think I'll be all right."

On weak legs she headed toward the Media Center on the second floor, where her study period was held. As she climbed the stairs the memory of her discovery flooded over her. She reached for the bald spot behind her left ear, but her arm froze in midair. Her books spilled down the steps and she sagged against the railing.

"Can I help you?" said a tall boy coming up the stairs behind her. She turned with a start, but the calm look on his face somehow comforted her. She didn't know his name but she thought he was new to Denniston High that fall.

He picked up her books as he climbed the steps. "Can I carry these for you? Where's your next class?"

Grateful for the boy's assistance, Meredith began to regain her composure. "Thanks. I have study hall in the Media Center," she said shyly.

"I'm going there too," he said simply and led her down the hall.

As they took seats at the first table in the room, Meredith looked at her companion. He was handsome in a mysterious way, with deep dark eyes and a mane of slightly unkempt black hair.

"I'm Meredith Turner."

"Colin Dorn," said the dark-haired boy. "You're running for Student Council, right?"

"So you've seen my signs," Meredith said, smiling. "You're new to school aren't you?"

"Yes," he answered simply.

"Where are you from?"

"The eastern part of the state."

"Really? What do your parents do?"

"My parents are dead."

"Oh. I'm sorry."

Colin answered Meredith's questions politely, but she got the impression he didn't much like talking about himself. Feeling more relaxed sitting beside him than she had all morning, Meredith opened the book she had to read for English class.

During the rest of the period Meredith couldn't help but glance at Colin every now and then. In appearance and demeanor he was very different from Kit, but she found something strangely attractive about the new boy. Maybe if she and Kit didn't get back together . . .

When Meredith said good-bye to Colin at the end of the period, her thoughts returned to the ominous note. She went through the rest of her morning classes not feeling quite herself. As the hours passed, she had the increasingly uneasy sensation that some force was guiding her along. Words came out of her mouth before she realized she'd spoken; gestures were completed without her realizing she'd moved. Meredith couldn't understand what was happening to her.

By lunchtime she was a jumble of exposed nerves. Outside the rain continued to fall, casting a dark, shadowless aura through the large plate-glass windows in the school cafeteria. She had to get to the bottom of it somehow, to discover what was making her feel so strange.

Kit will have the answer, she thought wildly as she got into the meal line. She needed desperately to talk to someone about what was happening. The handsome track star was practically her best friend, and despite their fight the day before, Meredith hoped he would help her figure this out. She surveyed the cafeteria in search of him, and a big lump formed in her throat. He was sitting with Suzy Gorham.

That hurt. Suzy had just about the worst reputation in the whole school, and from the looks of it, she wasn't wasting any time with Kit. She was looking at him as if she thought he was the most wonderful thing on earth, and from Meredith's vantage point he appeared to be smiling at her just as sweetly.

There was no way Meredith could bring herself to bare her soul to Kit with Suzy next to him. But she had to talk to someone. She looked around for Patti, Liz, and Missy. Meredith saw Liz and Patti at a table near the door, but Missy was nowhere in sight. Of all the days for her to be home sick, thought Meredith as she carried her tray to her friends' table.

"You'd think they'd serve something special today in honor of our distinguished candidates," Patti said, pointing to the unidentified concoction on her plate.

"It is special," Liz continued. "Premium quality Alpo. Or is it 9-Lives?"

"Very funny, girls," Meredith said, sitting down. She knew her friends had seen her troubled expression and were trying to cheer her up. But nothing could help. Not now.

Patti took a bite out of her meal and said, "I spent my entire study period thinking about that box. There's only one explanation. One of the other candidates must have put it there to scare you off."

"But who?" asked Liz, taking a sip from her carton of orange juice. "Kit?"

"Naw." Patti shook her head. "He may be a jerk for dumping Meredith, but he's also the most popular kid in the class. He wouldn't have to resort to a dumb stunt like that. It must have been Greg or Valerie."

"Not Greg," said Liz. "He's got the sympathy vote going for him." Greg Harper wasn't especially popular but he'd been badly hurt in a Moped accident last spring and had spent weeks in the hospital. He still used crutches and had to have another student carry his books from class to class.

"That leaves Valerie," Patti said, "though I've got to admit she seems too timid to do

32

something this crazy."

"You never know," Liz said plainly. "Sometimes the quiet, studious types are the ones you've got to watch out for. You never know what kind of evil is lurking in their minds."

"That's true," Patti interjected. "And we all know Valerie Haegstrom doesn't stand a ghost of a chance of winning with Meredith in the race. Right, Meredith?"

Meredith had been picking at her food, oblivious to the chatter of her friends. "What did you say?"

"We were talking about the mystery joker," said Patti.

"I've got news for you two," Meredith said tonelessly, staring at their faces. "It's no joke."

"Of course it is," challenged Patti. "Where's your sense of humor?"

"It's not a joke," Meredith repeated. "Come to the bathroom with me if you don't believe me."

She jumped to her feet and headed for the door. Mutely the two girls followed, exchanging questioning looks along the way. When they reached the privacy of the first-floor girls' bathroom, Meredith pulled aside her long, golden curls and pointed to the stubby patch behind her left ear.

"Explain what kind of joke that is!" she demanded, bursting into tears.

Liz and Patti were silent, but the expressions on their faces revealed the shock they both felt. Patti's eyes grew larger as she stared at Meredith.

"Oh no," she whispered. "Meredith, that's really strange."

"I'm sure there's a simple explanation," Liz said, pacing the black tiled floor. She'd already begun to recover the composure she was known for, and her brow was furrowed in thought. "Sure this seems spooky, but I don't think there's anything to be afraid of."

Meredith wiped her eyes. It made her feel better to get it out in the open with her two dear friends. Of course Liz was right. She was blowing this thing all out of proportion.

"What do you think happened?" Meredith asked Liz.

Liz sighed. "Can't say for sure. But I'll bet somebody you know—like Valerie—simply caught you off guard. You know, dozing in study hall or something. She's in your study, isn't she?"

Meredith nodded.

"See," Liz said triumphantly. "There's your culprit."

"Just the same, you'd better be careful," Patti added. "From now on don't go anywhere by yourself. Not anywhere. Make sure that Liz or I—or better yet both of us—are with you. Okay?"

"Yeah," Liz agreed. "There's nothing to worry about, but you know the old saying, safety in numbers."

"Okay," agreed Meredith. She tried to sound confident but a shadowy feeling crossed her mind, a feeling that told her she was all alone, a feeling that told her there was a definite connection between the hair and her peculiar dream. She closed her eyes for a moment and saw two blazing red dots. Fear welled up inside her. There was nothing her friends could do to help her now, she thought madly. She was all alone.

"Well, this is it," Meredith thought gloomily as she walked toward the gym an hour later. At the door she met Mr. Perkins, the white-haired government teacher who served as advisor to the Student Council.

"The juniors sit along there," he said, pointing to a group of four folding chairs up on stage.

Meredith's stomach tightened as she climbed up the steps and onto the platform. How could she possibly give her speech, especially after the dreadful morning she'd gone through! She dropped into the empty chair at one end of the junior section.

"Hi, Meredith," Kit said, his voice cautious. "How've you been?"

Her chance to talk to him had finally

come. Her heart was pounding and she knew her face was red, but she tried to smile. A few minutes remained before the assembly began. Maybe if she could explain to him the terrible terror that had come over her, she would be able to pull herself together for her speech. She needed him so much. But as she tried to put her feelings into words, she found herself saying, "I saw at lunch today that you're getting along fine without me." The venom in her voice surprised Meredith as much as it did Kit.

The blond-haired boy sighed and turned his head to the floor. "Suzy's just a friend."

"I'll bet," Meredith shot back at him.

Why was she saying such things? Meredith felt shaky and confused. She looked out at the crowd. The auditorium was filling up fast. Meredith felt her throat tighten as she remembered her botched history report. I've got to get a grip on myself, she thought. She shut her eyes but opened them again quickly when the two blood-red eyes from the night before filled her vision.

The faces of the students blurred before Meredith. Her classmates laughed and chattered as they waited for the assembly to begin. Meredith thought wistfully, how I wish I were one of them. A face in the crowd with nothing more on my mind than listen-

ing to a bunch of candidates being introduced. A face in the crowd. The words snag-
ged her thoughts and made her shiver. Fear
gripped her once again as she stared at the
sea of students. She couldn't stand up there
in front of them. Not now. Not alone.

But in that instant she could feel someone staring at her. Eyes peered into her
soul, commanding her to look at the audi-
ence without fear or panic. As if being led by
an invisible force, she let herself be mes-
merized by the shiny eyes that looked up at
her and held her gaze. They didn't spook
her now and she couldn't have looked away
if she had wanted to. She tried to make out
the face behind the eyes, but at that moment the room darkened and Mr. Perkins
walked to the center of the stage to begin
the assembly.

Entranced by the mysterious being in the
crowd, Meredith barely heard the teacher's
opening speech and was only dimly aware of
the freshmen and sophomores parading up
to the microphone to give their speeches. As
Mr. Perkins introduced the junior candidates a small thrill traveled through Meredith, a feeling of exhilaration she had never
before experienced. She felt dizzy and breathless, her breasts moving against her blouse.

Mr. Perkins called her name.

She wasn't afraid anymore.

Chapter Four

"It's the weirdest thing," Meredith told her mother and father that evening at dinner. "I honestly can't remember what happened at the assembly. Liz and Patti said I made a great impression with my speech, but I don't remember what I said at all." Meredith's hand unconsciously brushed the short bristly hairs behind her ear.

"You must have been too excited to

think," comforted her father. "It often happens to me when I have to give a presentation."

But it hadn't seemed like ordinary nervousness to Meredith. She had blacked out during the speech. Just like she had in French class. All she could remember was a feeling of utter peace, like floating in one of those sensory-deprivation tanks. Or the water in her dream.

"It was strange, like in a dream. I felt like I had been there before—" She broke off, her throat tightening as hysteria rose inside her.

"Yes, Meredith?" her mother prodded.

Meredith caught her breath. "I—I can't remember what I was going to say." She wanted to tell her parents about her dream and the vision with the bright red eyes. But something wouldn't let her.

"Meredith dear, are you sure you're not catching a cold?"

Meredith shook her head in frustration. It figured she'd say something like that. "No, Mother." She sighed and pushed her chair away from the table. Rising unsteadily she said, "Excuse me. I have to get ready. Liz and Patti will be here any minute."

Since the election was the following week, she planned to meet that night with her campaign advisors to discuss her strategy in the remaining days. She'd planned the get-together well before the dream and the strange events of the day, but now Meredith was especially glad they were coming over, as it would give her a chance to find out what she'd said, what had gone on in those few minutes she'd stood before the school. She couldn't remember a thing . . .

Her friends were of little help, though, unable to elaborate on the specifics of her speech—much to their astonishment.

"But you're as good as in," Patti said. She was sitting cross-legged on the floor between Liz and Meredith, sipping a Coke.

"You were absolutely spellbinding," Liz said exuberantly. "I didn't know you had it in you."

"Thanks. Me either," Meredith said. "Too bad Missy wasn't there. Have either of you been able to get her on the phone?"

"Not me," Patti said quietly. "The line's been busy ever since I got home."

"It's a little unusual, don't you think?" Meredith asked, concerned.

The girls looked at one another and grew silent.

At last Liz broke in. "But we're here to talk about you, Meredith, and your campaign. You did fine up there today, but so did the others. Take Greg, for instance. Don't count him out. He's making a strong play for the female vote. I saw him twice today leaning on a pair of girls while Pete North was dragging along the crutches."

"That's not fair," Patti complained. "He's taking advantage of his accident to get votes."

"All's fair in love and politics," said Meredith sourly.

"Maybe you should take up belly dancing and launch a counter-campaign for the male vote," Patti suggested.

Meredith laughed, imagining herself shimmying through the halls between classes in a skimpy costume and putting on spectacular performances in the lunchroom. Greg Harper could never top that!

Liz took a stack of records from their holder beneath Meredith's stereo and sorted through them casually. "I also saw Greg hanging around near your locker today," she said soberly. "I hate to mention it, but you didn't get any more notes or locks of hair this afternoon, did you?"

Meredith fought down a feeling of panic. "No. At least nothing was hanging on my locker. I didn't really look that carefully inside." She didn't tell her friends about the growing sensation of fear that made her spine tingle every time she flashed on the haunting words inside the box. Nor did she tell them that every time she closed her eyes she saw those two crimson dots at the end of a long black path. She wanted to tell her friends the whole story, to explain her feeling that somebody had some kind of power over her now. But it was all so strange — she was afraid they wouldn't believe her.

"I thought you didn't suspect Greg, Liz," Patti remarked.

"I suspect everyone, especially anyone who has a motive. Greg really wants to win, and everyone knows he's running third behind Meredith and Kit. Who knows what he might do next?"

"Come off it, Liz," Meredith said with a shrug. "You're making too much of it. Greg's not a kook. I think your theory about Valerie being the one makes more sense, if you want to know the truth." She tried to make her voice sound more confident than she felt.

"Speaking of kooks, I gotta tell you I can't stay late," said Patti. "Mom's gotten all paranoid over that escaped convict, and she wants me home early."

Meredith's phone rang and the girls quieted down as she reached to answer it. "Hello?" Meredith said tentatively. "Hi, Kit," she said, brightening. "Yes, thanks. I liked your speech too."

Liz and Patti looked at Meredith intently as she continued her conversation with Kit.

"You want to see me? You have something to tell me?" she whispered into the receiver, turning so her friends couldn't hear.

"Let me guess," Liz said to Patti, barely hiding the sarcasm in her voice. "Mr. Popularity's asking her to jump off Claymore Peak and she's gladly agreeing."

"What's your problem, Liz?" Patti asked. "I think it'd be wonderful if Meredith and Kit got back together."

"She won't take him back if she's got any pride," Liz said. "The guy dumped her flat for no good reason. She should at least make him crawl back to her."

"Cut the dramatics, Liz." Patti said. "I have a feeling that's not why he called." She glanced at Meredith, who was numbly replacing the phone in its cradle.

"What'd the track star want?" Liz asked directly.

Meredith turned to her friends, scarcely hiding the shock she felt. "He wanted to let me know that Missy is missing." Her voice quavered. "She hasn't been seen since yesterday."

Patti opened her mouth in shock. "She just . . . disappeared?"

"Nobody knows. Kit saw some police cars parked outside the Prices' house a little while ago. When he saw one of the cops come out, he asked him what was going on.

43

The cop told Kit that last night after dinner Missy told her parents she was going to the library to work on a paper. She never came home."

"That's not like her at all," Patti said.

"I hope she's all right," Liz said, thinking of the convict still at large.

The girls fell silent as they thought about Missy. Meredith considered telling her friends that Kit had also asked her to meet him the next day to talk about something. She hoped he wanted to get back together, but she knew if she mentioned it, Liz would give her a hard time.

At last Liz turned to Patti and said, "I don't know about you, but I've got tons of homework to do tonight. I have a book report due tomorrow on a book I haven't even finished reading yet, and Biology Bob is really pouring it on lately. I'll be up until midnight at least."

"Me too," said Patti, checking her watch. "I've got to call Mom and tell her I'm on my way. We'll see you tomorrow, Meredith. I'll call downstairs."

After the girls left, Meredith closed the door behind them, turned off the lights, and sat motionless for a long time. She looked out her window, trancelike, as the dark shadows of night began to obscure all traces of moonlight from the starless sky.

She had homework too, but she was too upset to concentrate on it. She didn't feel like doing anything; instead she leaned back against the side of her bed, resting her head on the soft coverlet and thinking about the being who seemed to have her under its spell. Who are you? she wanted to shout. What do you want from me?

Before she realized it Meredith was asleep, and within seconds her dream returned. As before, she was irresistibly drawn to the cobblestone path, but for some reason this time she wasn't afraid. She was, in fact, glad to be there, almost as if she'd been invited by someone special. A soft blanket of mist enfolded her and caressed her cheeks. She traced her lips with her tongue and felt full and open.

Ahead of her on the path was a figure, but she couldn't tell who it was. The fog was too thick. The figure was calling her name, however, beckoning her to come.

"I'm on my way," she called as she hurried forward. "Wait for me. Wait."

The figure seemed to be standing still as it motioned to her, but no matter how fast she walked, she could get no closer.

"MEREDITH . . ."

"I'm coming! Wait!"

She started to run and soon was breathless. The figure was still far away. Pushing the strands of mist aside, she peered into the darkness. If only she could see who it was, see who this person was she wanted to be with almost as much as life itself. Tears streamed down her face as she struggled on.

"Wait," she cried. "Wait."

"MEREDITH ... MEREDITH ... MEREDITH ..."

Just as she came almost close enough to recognize the figure, the dream ended and she awoke. Exhausted, she lay there and let the memory of the experience flood over her.

Kit. It had to be Kit, she thought, trying to make sense of the dream. It was Kit who'd spoken to her last, Kit who'd said he had something important to tell her, Kit who she wanted to be with so badly. Kit has the power over me, she concluded, a chill rising up her spine. But what it meant she did not know.

Chapter Five

Meredith could scarcely keep her eyes open at breakfast the next morning. Sitting down at the table, she spread butter on two pieces of toast and stared off into space, letting her food turn cold.

She was drained from the latest dream and more desperate than ever to understand what was happening to her. If only she could have seen the face of the person calling her. In the black of night, she had been certain it was Kit. But in sober daylight, questions kept floating in her mind. If it really was Kit, why didn't he reveal himself to her? And why would he want her under his spell?

The vision of the misty cobblestone path filled her head. She caught her breath, trying to piece things together. The scene had been the same as in the first dream she'd had the night before. It had been dark in both dreams, dark and foggy, and she hadn't been able to see the figure that called to her. Yet she felt drawn to it, compelled against her will to challenge anything to be with it. It could have been anyone, even a madman, and she would have gone to him. But the dream left her no clue to his identity.

"You look tired this morning, Meredith." The sound of her father's voice startled her. He put down his morning paper and poured himself a second cup of coffee. "Studying late again?"

Meredith stifled a yawn. "No, Dad. I just had a dream. It—" She couldn't go on, she couldn't get the words out.

"Not a nightmare, I hope?" her mother asked. "I know how upset you must be about Missy."

The thought of Missy's disappearance set Meredith even more on edge. What was going on? She needed to tell her parents about the dream. Maybe they could help her find a logical explanation.

But as she opened her mouth she heard herself say evenly, "No, it wasn't a nightmare." She stood up abruptly, feeling an inexplicable need to get away from her parents, and reached for her corduroy jacket. "I've got to go now."

Meredith covered the seven blocks from the Turner house to Denniston High in record time. In spite of the dream and her exhaustion, she felt anxious to get to school, as if something was drawing her there. Some unseen force told her she would find an answer there.

The building was deserted when she arrived, making the cavernous hallways look more intimidating than usual. But for some reason Meredith wasn't afraid as she drew near her locker.

She spun the combination on her lock and pulled the locker door open. An envelope lay on top of her books. Meredith frowned. It hadn't been there when she left school the day before, and nobody, not even her best friends, knew the combination.

A feeling of dreadful excitement came over her as she reached for the unsealed letter. She unfolded the piece of paper and let out a gasp as she read the words written there in crimson-colored ink: DO NOT LISTEN TO THE WORDS OF INSINCERE FOOLS. THEY DO NOT HAVE YOUR INTERESTS AT HEART. LISTEN TO ME. YOU ARE IN MY POWER.

Meredith stared down at the paper. Her hands were trembling so that the bold letters seemed to dance before her like fiery demons. Hastily she crumpled the sheet and took a deep breath, trying to slow her racing heart. But the feeling of panic wouldn't go away.

There has to be a simple explanation for this, she told herself as she rubbed the stubby patch behind her ear. Closing the locker door, she forced herself to study its dents and scratch marks, as if by concentrating on them she could erase the presence of this second note. The olive-drab paint was chipped and dozens of initials had been scratched into its surface over the years. The vent holes were small and round, making the locker look as if it had been hit by a blast of buckshot. Meredith found no relief. There were no clues there. It had been locked, and there was no earthly way anyone could have gotten inside without getting the combination from her. Yet someone had. But there was no earthly way she thought, shuddering.

Somewhere down the hall a floorboard

creaked. Meredith whirled around, terrified. The sight of a heavy-set boy carrying
a trombone case made her relax
momentarily. He stopped beside a locker at
the far end of the corridor, and a moment
later he disappeared down the stairs. She
was alone again on the silent third floor.

Smoothing out the paper, Meredith
looked at the message again. She had to
find a clue. The letters had been made with
a broad-tipped red marker, the same kind of
marker she'd used to make her student
council posters. The same kind of marker
used by Greg . . . or Valerie . . . or Kit.

LISTEN TO ME, the message said. Meredith
felt a shock of electricity through her body.
What did it mean?

"Meredith!" Patti's voice startled her. "Did
you hear?" From Patti's pained expression,
Meredith feared it was terrible news.

"What are you talking about? Something
to do with Missy?"

"No," Patti said. "It's worse. Mr. Stevens,
the old biology teacher. They found him
dead this morning!"

"Mr. Stevens? How'd it happen?"

"He drowned. They found him in Hadley
Pond."

"How awful!"

"They think it could have been murder. It
sure doesn't make sense that an old man

like him would have gone for a swim this time of year." She shivered.

Meredith was silent. She didn't know why, but she felt Mr. Stevens' death was a portent of more evil to come.

"Do you think it's got anything to do with Missy?" Patti asked.

Meredith had a terrible feeling the two events were connected — and that they had something to do with her dreams. But how could she explain her certainty to Patti?

"Maybe it's the work of that escaped lunatic," Patti went on. "It's creepy."

The girls grew silent as they got their books out of their lockers. As they walked together to homeroom Meredith opened her mouth to tell Patti about the latest note. But something told her not to.

Meredith was surprised not to see Madame Dussault standing outside her classroom. It was the first time in the three years she'd had her that Meredith could recall the tiny woman being absent. Meredith felt uneasy as she took her usual seat at the back of the room.

The class passed more quickly than she'd expected. The dour young man who substituted had obviously never studied French and amused the class with his fractured pronunciations. After a while he gave up completely, turning the class into a study period and letting the students get rowdy.

But despite the commotion, Meredith couldn't forget the note she'd found in her locker. She was overwhelmed by a haunting feeling. Thoughts swirled in her head. The dreams, the lock of hair, her mysterious blackouts, Missy's disappearance, and now Mr. Stevens' death. It was too much for her. She felt as if she were trapped in a gigantic spider web. YOU ARE IN MY POWER, the first note said. LISTEN TO ME, said the second. Panic rose inside Meredith. I'm trapped—trapped like a fly in a web, and there's nothing I can do to get out!

Suddenly she remembered that she'd given Kit her combination during the first week of school. So maybe it was Kit. Maybe there was a rational explanation. It wasn't enough for him to leave her, he had to torture her with these notes. Meredith was on the verge of tears. I've got to get to the bottom of this, thought Meredith. She'd speak to him at lunchtime. She calmed down a little. Hadn't he told her last night he wanted to talk to her? He had to listen. She had to find out what was going on.

The bell rang and Meredith hurried into the hall.

"Meredith, wait up."

Meredith frowned as she slowed and looked over her shoulder. It was Francine

Cohen, a senior and one of the reporters for the Denniston High *Echo*. Terribly overweight, she was panting heavily as she raced up the hall.

"Do you have a minute?" she asked breathlessly.

Meredith looked at her strangely. "How did you know where to find me?"

"Intuition," Francine answered. "I'm interviewing all the candidates for the paper. I'd like to get your opinions on some of the issues that will be facing the Student Council this year."

"Gee, Francine, I'd love to talk to you, but I'm in a terrible hurry right now." Meredith tried to keep all traces of irritation out of her voice. She didn't know why, but something was tugging her away from Francine and pulling her in the direction of the Media Center. "There's something important I have to do now. How about after school, okay?" she asked, stepping up her pace.

"Great," Francine called after her. "I'll meet you at the front door. We can go across the street and have a soda. My treat." Meredith didn't hear any more as she hurried along to the wood-framed double doors at the end of the hall.

The Media Center was large and there must have been a hundred students spread out among the tables between the bookshelves. She slipped into an empty chair and opened her computer math book. She didn't bother to look up and, tearing a sheet out of her notebook, she began going over the problems from yesterday's lesson. Vaguely she became aware of another person taking a seat across from her, and she grew uneasy. Finally she looked up—right into Valerie Haegstrom's smiling face. A smile that looked eerily twisted.

Quickly Meredith gathered her books and moved to the first empty seat she could find, feeling dizzy and strangely disoriented. Valerie's face had evoked that queasy fear she'd been running away from. As soon as she took the new seat she felt much calmer.

"Hi, Meredith."

Startled, Meredith looked up at the boy sitting across from her. Colin Dorn.

"I'm sorry I frightened you," he said, smiling.

"Oh, no." Meredith sighed. "It wasn't you. This just hasn't been my day." She looked at the dark-haired boy and smiled back at him.

"I wouldn't think a girl like you could have any troubles."Colin said.

"Well, I do," she found herself saying.

Colin blushed slightly. "I heard your speech yesterday. It was not the speech of a troubled girl."

"Thanks." Meredith felt herself relaxing a bit.

"In fact, if I were a junior I'd vote for you." Colin shot her a half smile. "Are you worried about the election?"

"No," Meredith said. "It's something you wouldn't understand." Meredith looked into Colin's deep, dark eyes and had the stange feeling he was flirting with her. If Kit really was playing these tricks on her, she certainly didn't want him back. Maybe she and Colin would get together . . .

She felt a warm tingle. Colin was a very attractive boy, she thought, with his handsome features, thick shock of black hair, and friendly smile. She thought the black turtleneck he wore was especially flattering to his swarthy complexion.

"Maybe I wouldn't understand," Colin said after a while. "But I can tell you this. You have nothing to worry about."

"What makes you say that?"

"Sometimes I can tune into these things."

"Really? Like ESP?"

"Something like that," he said pleasantly.

Maybe Colin could help her figure out the dream. "Can you read minds?" she asked hesitantly, more to tease him than anything else.

"Sometimes," he answered, smiling coyly.

"Okay, tell me what I'm thinking."

Meredith concentrated hard on the two luminescent eyes she remembered from her dream. If he could see them, she thought, maybe he could also visualize the person behind the eyes. She shuddered when they came into view; they were as clear as if they were right before her, although the face was as murky as ever.

"Are you thinking real hard?" Colin asked.

"Yes."

Meredith thought she saw something flicker in Colin's expression, and for a moment her heart soared at the possibility he saw them too. But then he told her, "Sorry, I'm not reading anything. I guess this isn't my day either."

"Thanks for trying," she said. "Anyway I feel better now."

"If I can be of any help, don't hesitate to ask," he said.

Just then the bell rang and Meredith headed for the cafeteria feeling better than she had all day. She would talk to Kit and clear everything up. But scanning the lunchroom for the track star, she couldn't find him, although she did catch sight of Patti and Liz, who were waving at her from a table in the far corner.

Meredith nodded back and glanced at the door just in time to see Kit walk in. But he wasn't alone. There was Suzy Gorham by his side, just like the day before. Meredith's heart sank. She needed so much to talk to Kit—alone. Jealousy swept through her, flushing her cheeks.

Meredith swallowed hard and carried her tray to the table where Patti and Liz sat. Her friends had seen the look on her face and knew Meredith was upset about seeing Kit with Suzy.

"Don't look now," Patti said, trying to form the words without moving her mouth. "But they aren't sitting together."

"Who cares who Kit Van Leer sits with?" Meredith hissed.

Still, throughout lunch Meredith watched Kit out of the corner of her eye. He was sitting with Bill Hollingsworth, Curt Lockwood and Dan Means, all members of the track team. Suzy Gorham was several tables away. When Kit got up to leave, Meredith made an excuse about needing to get her chemistry book out of her locker before the bell rang, and hurried after him, She wasn't sure why she had lied to Patti and Liz, or even why she hadn't told them about the second note. Perhaps after she talked to Kit and got everything out in the open, she would be able to confide in her friends.

She found Kit taping up a corner of a

campaign poster which had come undone. Despite her growing annoyance with him, she couldn't help noticing how handsome he looked, so tall and athletic, with his blond hair brushed casually across his forehead. It had been a long time since they'd had an extended conversation face to face, and Meredith found herself suddenly nervous as she approached.

"Kit?" she asked hesitantly. Her own voice sounded strange and far away.

"Well if it isn't my biggest competition," he said. "Are you the one who sabotaged this poster?"

"Very funny, Kit," she said sarcastically. Kit's smile slowly began to ebb.

"I need to talk to you about something important," she continued. "It's scaring me half to death, and I think you know what it is."

"You mean old man Stevens and Missy? I know, it's pretty creepy."

"Scarier than that even," she said.

"Scarier? What are you talking about?"

"You know very well what I'm talking about. The box hanging on the front of my locker yesterday. The box with the lock of my hair. The note that said: YOU ARE IN MY POWER."

Meredith paused, waiting for Kit's reaction. He narrowed his eyes and shook his head slowly. Then he cupped her face in his hands. "Meredith, you're letting this whole thing with Missy spook you. Don't you know a gag when you see one?"

She took a deep breath, then turned her head and pointed to the spot behind her ear. "You call this a gag?"

Kit shrugged. "Are you sure you didn't do it to yourself? In any case, it doesn't look like anything worth getting upset about. If you want my advice, forget it."

"It figures you'd say that." Meredith tried to control her voice, and fight her own rising feeling of panic. Of course Kit would try to make her think it was something else. He had to, she rationalized. Still she continued, "This morning when I got to school and opened my locker, there was an envelope inside. It wasn't there yesterday after school. I know it wasn't. There was a message inside. Would you mind explaining this?"

Meredith pulled the note out of her history book and thrust it at Kit. He took the paper and as he read it a bemused smile played across his lips.

"You think I wrote this?" he asked. "Come on, Meredith, you told me yourself your locker was locked."

"But you're the only other person who knows my combination," she insisted.

"Really, Meredith, it wasn't me. I don't

know what any of this is about." He looked at her earnestly.

Was Kit telling the truth? She'd been so sure he had to be the one playing tricks on her. But she saw the concerned look in his eyes. Maybe it wasn't him. The room seemed to spin around Meredith and her stomach grew queasy as that awful black fear enveloped her again. What's going on? Am I going crazy? she thought hysterically.

Meredith whirled around and raced for the girls' bathroom. Locking herself in a stall, she leaned against the door and began to sob. What's happening to me? she wondered over and over. She heard a voice echo in her mind: YOU ARE IN MY POWER.

Chapter Six

It was a long time before Meredith felt calm enough to leave the bathroom. As she opened the door into the hall she noted with a start that the school had grown quiet. Looking at her wristwatch, she realized that afternoon classes had been underway for ten minutes. She hadn't even heard the bell.

She couldn't bear going to her math class. Instead, she tiptoed upstairs to her locker, got her books, and slipped into the Media Center. It was easy enough to hide out there until the end of school.

When the afternoon dismissal bell rang, Meredith decided to wait until most of the students had left for the day before going to her locker. She was still too shaky to face anyone.

Gradually the after-school sounds ebbed as the halls emptied. When she thought most of the students had left, she hurried through the deserted halls to her locker, where she pitched her books inside and grabbed her jacket off the hook. Then she remembered she was supposed to meet with Francine, and although she knew she had an obligation to talk to the newspaper reporter, the idea of spending half an hour with her was more than Meredith could stand. Tomorrow she'd tell Francine she'd forgotten all about their appointment, that she'd been preoccupied worrying about Missy.

Meredith avoided the front of the building, where Francine would be growing impatient by now. She left by one of the back doors, the door beside the wood shop because it led to the faculty parking lot and few students ever went out that way.

She pushed the creaky door open and gasped. There at the end of the long alleyway that led to the parking lot were two ruby eyes begging her to come closer.

"No," she screamed. "Go away!" Holding her books tight to her chest, Meredith ran back into the school, along the long empty corridors, and down the front steps past an astonished-looking Francine. Despite her fatigue, she ran as fast as she could, until at last she reached the front door of her house. Panting heavily, she jumbled her key in the lock, opened the door, then slammed it behind her with all her might.

But she could still feel the eyes staring relentlessly at her.

An hour later Meredith was startled by the ring of the telephone. It was Patti.

"Meredith, are you okay?" Patti asked. "Where were you after school? Liz and I looked all over for you."

Meredith sighed deeply and answered, "My head was throbbing, so I decided to come home early. A couple of aspirins and a nap, and I'm as good as new."

"Are you sure you're all right? You don't sound normal."

"I'm fine," she mumbled. "I just got up from a nap, that's all."

"If you say so," Patti said. "I was just wondering what was up with you and Kit. From the way he was growling at everybody in Basic Business last period, I thought maybe you two had a fight or something."

Suddenly a strange feeling came over Meredith. "I've decided Kit's all wrong for me. He's not the kind of guy I really want to go steady with."

Patti sounded puzzled. "That's a funny thing for you to say. Two days ago you loved him."

"For your information, I'm interested in Colin Dorn." The certainty in her voice startled Meredith. What had come over her? Colin had been nice to her and she did find him attractive, but they barely knew each other.

"Colin Dorn? That new boy? Gosh, Meredith, he's so—" Patti tried to be tactful. "He's so quiet and he doesn't hang around with the rest of the kids. I always thought he was kind of—odd."

"Colin's a very sensitive boy. Much nicer than Mr. Popularity Van Leer," Meredith shot back, surprised at her tone of voice. She didn't understand what was making her say such things. She'd better get off the phone before she said something even crazier.

"I've got a test to study for, Patti. I'll see you tomorrow."

As she dropped the receiver into the cradle she half heard Patti say something about taking another nap and maybe she'd come to her senses. Come to her senses. She'd been trying to get a grip on herself for the past two days, but she couldn't even seem to control the words that came out of her own mouth. *I really must be going crazy,* she thought, hysteria mounting inside her. *I wish I could explain this whole thing to someone, but I can't trust myself to speak at all.* A cold fear swallowed her and she stared, trancelike, out the window.

When the phone rang again just before dinner, Meredith went right on setting the table and made no move to answer it. Her mother, used to Meredith jumping for the phone on the first ring, gave her a surprised look and answered it herself.

"It's for you," she said, offering the receiver to Meredith. "It's Kit."

"Tell him I don't want to talk to him," she said coldly.

Meg Turner frowned. "I'm sorry, Kit. She can't come to the phone. Is there a message I can take?" She listened for a moment and then turned back to Meredith. "Honey, he says it's very important. Won't you talk to him?"

"No, Mother. Tell him I'm sick. Tell him anything you want, but I'm not coming to the phone." Meredith could feel forces inside her feeding the vehemence she put into those words. She never wanted to have anything to do with Kit again.

Flustered, her mother made some excuse about Meredith not feeling well and took the message. "Oh, no!" she cried into the receiver after hearing Kit's words. Hanging up, she turned to Meredith.

"Honey, I've got some terrible news. Kit wanted to let you know before you heard it elsewhere." She paused. "They found Missy Price late this afternoon. She's dead, Meredith. They found her body at the lake in Claymore Park."

Meredith calmly took the cloth napkins from the china closet and placed them around the table. She had heard every word her mother said, but her expression bore no trace of understanding. A voice inside her told her that Missy's death was of no concern to her.

That night Meredith had another dream. Once again she was deep within a misty vastness, almost as if she were suspended in another dimension. There were no cobblestone paths this time, no natural landmarks she could identify—just an endless vacuum lit at one end by the fire from the now familiar jeweled eyes. After a while she felt the mist dissipating, gradually revealing a faded carpet at her feet. She was in a room of some sort, a theater, she realized after a while. But it was unlike any theater she'd ever been in.

Slowly she glided down the center aisle, past rows of ancient wooden seats covered with faded, torn cushions. They were empty, except for one seat at the far end of the first row.

Meredith picked up her pace, suddenly driven toward a rendezvous with the person waiting there. She had no idea who it was — all she could see was a dark head staring at the blank movie screen before him.

At last she made it to the front row and found her heart soaring when she saw who it was: Colin Dorn. He smiled back at her and invited her to join him for the next showing. She did so willingly . . . and it was only then that she noticed Kit at the opposite end of the row, a vague but clearly disapproving figure in a shadowy landscape.

Chapter Seven

"It's just awful, isn't it?"

Patti ran up to Meredith at the locker banks the following morning. Meredith was slowly looking through her locker for messages. There were none.

"What are you talking about?" she asked disinterestedly.

"Missy," Patti said. "I tried to call you last night to tell you, but your father said you couldn't come to the phone."

"Oh, yes, I heard the news," Meredith responded without much emotion, reaching for her books.

"Meredith, how can you be so calm? Missy was your friend. I—I still can't believe she's gone."

"It is sad. But these things happen for reasons we must accept." At the edge of her mind an uneasiness tugged at Meredith. She didn't know why she said those words, why she didn't feel more sorrow over her friend's death. But she was enveloped in a trancelike calm and didn't dwell on thoughts of Missy.

"And to think that new boy found her. Of all the people."

"New boy?" Meredith turned to face Patti.

"Yes. Your friend Colin." Patti gave her a quizzical look.

"Colin found her?" At the sound of his name Meredith felt her heart flutter.

"Yes. I went over to the Prices' as soon as I heard. Mr. Price told me that Colin found her yesterday afternoon at the lake. The police took him in for questioning and had him there for hours."

"Do they think he, uh, had something to do with her death?" she asked, showing sudden concern.

Patti wrinkled her nose. "No . . . although I told you he was strange . . ." Patti's voice

70

trailed off as she saw Meredith glaring at her.

"I'm really surprised at you, Patti. You don't even know the boy and you're suggesting he —" Meredith broke off, indignant.

"It's just that he doesn't seem to have many friends. Nobody seems to know much about him."

"That's because he's very shy and if you think that's strange, I feel sorry for you. I think he's very sweet and gentle." A thrill went through Meredith as she remembered her latest dream.

Patti looked at Meredith strangely. "In any case, I heard they found a note by the lake. Nobody's saying what's in it, but whatever it was, it was enough to get your friend off the hook." She paused. "Just be careful, Meredith."

Meredith didn't respond. Instead, she collected her books from her locker, gently replacing the lock in its hole. Without so much as calling good-bye to Patti, she walked down the hall to her homeroom. For some reason, she couldn't get Colin out of her mind. Just thinking about him gave her a feeling of peace, a sense of security. Maybe now she could depend on Colin to protect her, to shield her from the evil that was chasing her mercilessly.

She couldn't wait to get to the Media

Center and wasn't surprised to find an empty seat waiting for her next to Colin. His eyes shone brightly as he looked closely at her.

"Hello," she said, taking the seat.

Colin looked up from his book. "I'm happy to see you, Meredith."

"I heard you found Missy." she said, her eyes full of concern. "It must have been awful ..."

Colin looked at his hands, clasped together on the table. "It was. But it had to be done."

"How did you find her?"

"Like I told you, I sometimes get these feelings. One came to me yesterday. I found myself being drawn to the park, drawn to that spot where ..." Colin bowed his head, unable to say anything more.

Meredith touched his shoulder. "I'm sorry, it must have been a frightening experience."

"I hope you never have to know," he answered, giving her a strange look. He went back to his homework at that point, so Meredith left him alone and picked up one of her own books. Still, she couldn't help casting a glance at him occasionally throughout the period. Gazing at his delicate chiseled nose and soft, smooth skin, she thought he looked vulnerable —

innocent. And yet he'd gone through the awful experience of finding a dead girl's body. Meredith found herself wanting to comfort him, to be the one to give him pleasure and reassurance after the macabre experience of discovering Missy's corpse. Her thoughts were so occupied with Colin she didn't even stop to remember that Missy had been her good friend.

After school Meredith walked down the front steps only to be accosted by Francine Cohen, who'd been lumbering around the building's edge carrying books stacked up to her chin. Obviously angry, she shouted, "Meredith Turner, what's your problem? You've been avoiding me."

"Oh, no," muttered Meredith under her breath. She knew she should talk to Francine for the sake of the election. The election. After the odd events of the past two days, she had hardly thought about it.

"I'm sorry, Francine. Let's do the interview now," said Meredith, suddenly anxious to talk about something normal, to forget about the strange experiences of the past days.

"Okay." The heavy-set girl's face softened. "Let's go to the Pop Shoppe. We can talk on the way."

But as they walked along the street,

Meredith couldn't concentrate on the reporter's questions. It was as if her mind had suddenly turned to cotton. She couldn't say anything and her eyes went blank.

"Meredith," Francine said insistently. "I was just asking you what you thought of — " She looked up at Meredith's pale face. "Are you all right? You look terrible. Hey, we can do this some other time ..." Her voice trailed off.

"I—I think I'm coming down with a headache. I don't feel quite myself," Meredith mumbled. "I'll call you after dinner."

"Okay," said Francine, giving her a strange look and hurrying away.

Suddenly Meredith was alone. She'd almost blacked out again. She felt dizzy and confused. Slowly she walked down the streets toward home. Maybe there she could find safety and shelter from the force that seemed to have her under its control. . . .

"Meredith, can I walk with you?"

The voice was soothing and made Meredith smile. "Sure, Colin, I'd like that," she said, turning to face the boy as he came up from behind.

Together they walked along in silence for several blocks. To Meredith, Colin seemed content just being with her. Meredith felt an unexpected wave of excitement. It was a wonderful sensation, something she'd never experienced before. Colin was so strong, so steady, someone to lean on. Not at all like Kit, who was more concerned with his popularity than anything else. Why had it taken her so long to find a boy as caring and mature as Colin?

Meredith was the first to break the silence. "I'm not dating Kit anymore."

Colin smiled. "I know. That's why I asked if I could walk with you. I'd like to take you out tomorrow night."

"I'd love to go with you," Meredith replied. Yes, Colin was the boy for her. She'd never felt so happy. And to think he was interested in her too.

"Can I sign you up for my campaign staff?" she teased.

At the mention of the election, Colin stopped and spun toward her. He bent over her, staring at her with brooding eyes. He put his hand under her chin and tilted her face toward his. A shiver of longing raced through her body.

"Kit Van Leer is going to win the election," he said evenly.

"Is that another one of your visions?" She turned away shyly, afraid to admit the sudden flash of desire she felt for him. "Besides, there are two Student Council seats open," she said lightly.

He looked into her eyes and said, "I want you." He lowered his lips to hers and kissed her hard.

Meredith responded willingly. She felt hypnotized, as if she were spinning in space, round and round, deeper and deeper into a dark void. Only the glow of Colin's presence and the power of his magnetism guided her. There was an unspoken understanding between them, something powerful that Meredith had never felt before.

Something snapped inside of her. She felt a sudden release from the tension of the past three days. She had found peace at last. She was in love. Meredith knew she wanted nothing but to be with Colin forever. She knew what she had to do. What were school politics compared to spending every moment she could with him?

Their lips parted. Meredith had no idea how much time passed as they gazed into one another's eyes. At last Colin slipped his arm around her shoulder, and she huddled against his strong, firm body as they continued toward her house.

When they arrived at the end of her driveway, Colin turned to her and said, "I'll see you tomorrow at school."

"Sure." She smiled. "Actually I'll be going in a little early in the morning to take care of a couple of things." She didn't tell him about the decision she'd just made, but she had a feeling he'd approve.

That evening Meredith kept her promise and called Francine. "I don't have time to talk now," she told the reporter. "But meet me tomorrow morning at my locker and I promise to have some very important news for you."

Relieved by the decision she'd made, Meredith slept heavily that night, and the next morning she dashed out of the house without eating breakfast. She knew what she had to do and didn't want to waste a minute.

Walking up and down the halls, she searched for campaign posters that read: MEREDITH TURNER FOR JUNIOR STUDENT COUNCIL REP, and ripped every one of them from the walls.

Chapter Eight

Other students were beginning to arrive at school. As they sauntered toward their lockers most of them paid little attention to Meredith, but a few looked at her with genuine surprise.

"Meredith Turner, what on earth are you doing?" Francine Cohen asked as she hurried up behind her.

"I'm withdrawing from the Student Council election. That's my news for you," she answered coolly.

"But why?" demanded Francine. "You're a cinch to win one of the seats."

"I don't have time to bother with it anymore," Meredith said abruptly. She moved on down the hall, leaving the bewildered Francine standing alone.

Meredith was feeling very calm and peaceful since she'd made her decision. Student Council would take up so much of her time. She'd rather spend those valuable hours working on her budding relationship with Colin. She looked around the hallway wondering where he was, hoping he'd be pleased with her decision.

There were twelve posters in all and she folded each one neatly as she pulled it down, planning to deposit all of them in the large trash basket outside the door to the office when she finished collecting them. As she moved into the section of corridor where the last poster hung, she stopped. Her heart leapt as she saw Kit leaning against the wall beside her poster with his hands shoved deep into the pockets of his varsity letter jacket. He was obviously waiting for her and wore a black, brooding expression.

"Francine just told me you're going around pulling down your posters and you're dropping out of the election," he said solemnly. "It isn't true, is it?"

"I'm afraid it is," she said, avoiding his eyes. "Now if you'll step aside, I'd like to take down that poster." She tried to sound determined.

Kit stared at her and didn't move. The dark look that had been on his face a moment before was gone, replaced by one of concern. "It's because of that guy Colin, isn't it?"

"How did you know?"

"I saw the two of you together yesterday. I hope you know what you're doing." Sighing deeply, he took her small hand in his strong one and gently pulled her toward him.

Part of Meredith wanted to be held in those familiar arms once more. She shivered, feeling a conflict tear her apart inside. Why was he coming on to her now? She'd done what he wanted. She'd bowed out of his life. She'd shifted her allegiance to Colin. Colin. The thought of him gave her the strength to resist Kit's advances.

"You don't have to worry about me anymore, Kit," she said. "I used to think you and I were right for each other and that being on the Student Council with you would be great, but I've changed my mind."

"That doesn't sound like you," Kit argued. "You haven't been acting like yourself lately," he said with concern.

For an instant her old feelings for Kit

began to rise inside her again. But then a blinding pain filled her head.

MEREDITH! called the voice she recognized from her dreams. Something gripped her will and bent it so she had no control. The room began to spin and Meredith couldn't keep Kit's face in focus.

"Meredith, Meredith!" Kit cried in terror. "What's wrong with your eyes!"

She felt something pulling her away from him. Dropping the posters at Kit's feet, she turned and ran, feeling as if a force outside her was powering her limbs. Meredith raced down the corridor, bumping into other students as she ran through the crowd. She heard Kit call after her, but she couldn't answer. Something told her she had to get away from him at all costs.

Out of breath, Meredith reached her locker. She gasped as she saw another tiny box dangling from the latch. With shaking hands she opened it. Written there in a blood-red scrawl were the words: YOUR FRIENDS ARE OUT TO BETRAY YOU. GET THEM OUT OF YOUR LIFE.

Later that morning at the Media Center Meredith was glad to see Colin approach her. His face was masked in shadows as he came near, although she could see his lean torso ripple in and out of the light as he worked his way through the maze of tables and chairs.

Meredith looked into the depths of his eyes. "I'm dropping out of the Student Council race," she told him.

His face seemed to soften at her words. "You did the right thing."

Meredith left the Media Center early to stop by Mr. Perkins' classroom. She was relieved to find him there, sitting at his desk grading papers from a sophomore government exam. He looked up when she approached the desk, smiled, and took off his glasses, laying them aside.

"Good morning, Meredith," he said pleasantly. "What can I do for you today?"

"I'm going to have to withdraw from the Student Council election," she said without hesitation. "I really have a heavy class load and with so much—"

"That's all right, my dear." Mr. Perkins smiled as he cut her off.

The teacher's response caught Meredith by surprise. She'd prepared a whole speech for him. "I'm glad you understand," she muttered.

"Think nothing of it," he said. "I know how busy you popular girls are with your boys. Go on now, and let someone who really wants the job have it."

Meredith left Mr. Perkins' room puzzled

but relieved to have gotten the chore over with. She still had some explaining to do, though, to Patti and Liz, and that might be hard—especially where Liz was concerned.

She decided to talk to them at lunch. Meredith reached the double doors to the cafeteria and spotted Patti and Liz entering the lunchroom from the gym.

"Meredith Turner," Patti said breathlessly. "What's this about you dropping out of the Student Council election? It's all over school!"

Liz didn't say anything, but the same question was written in her eyes.

"It's true," Meredith admitted. "As of this morning I am no longer a candidate." She smiled as she thought of Colin, the reason for her decision. A look of satisfaction spread over her face.

"But why?" asked Liz. "You really wanted to win. You didn't get another message from that nut, did you?"

The thought of the lastest note made Meredith shudder. She started to tell her friends but instead heard her voice say, "I told Mr. Perkins I didn't have time, and he was just as glad to see me withdraw."

"That's not surprising," Patti cut in bitterly. "Valerie Haegstrom's his niece. With you out of the race she's got a fighting chance."

Meredith considered that fact for a moment, then continued. "Actually I dropped out so I could spend more time with my new boyfriend."

"And who would that be?" Liz asked, perturbed.

"Colin Dorn. In fact, I'm meeting him for lunch." She hadn't planned to eat with Colin, but suddenly Meredith knew he would want to be with her. Feeling a new sense of triumph she watched as stunned looks appeared on both of her friends' faces.

"But what about Kit?" asked Patti. "You really weren't kidding when you said you didn't want to see him anymore."

"No, I wasn't," she said emphatically.

Liz looked at her narrowly. "What's going on, Meredith? I've never seen you act so strange."

"I explained it all to Patti yesterday. Kit is dull, boring, and conceited. He doesn't really care about anything except playing the big man. I've had it with that routine, it's too dumb. For a long time now I've been looking for someone who is more mature, someone who cares about me for what I am, not because I can win some kids' election. Colin's that person—and there's nothing you or Patti can say that will change my mind."

"How can you say that? Just what do you know about Colin? How can you be sure he's so perfect? Everybody thinks he's odd. And his being the one to find Missy just doesn't sit well with me. If I were you, I'd stay away from him."

"Yeah, he's a pretty creepy person to hang around with," Patti agreed.

"Since when have you become an expert on boys?" Meredith glared at her overweight friend. "You don't even date."

"That's hitting below the belt," Liz said in Patti's defense.

"And since when are you so all-knowing and all-wise?" Meredith harped at Liz. "You don't know anything."

"Let's get our lunch trays and go find a table where we can talk about this privately," Liz whispered. "We're starting to draw a crowd."

Meredith glanced around. Several nearby students were apparently listening to their conversation. She glared at Dan Means, who looked uneasy for a moment and then moved on. "You'll have to go through without me," Meredith said. "I'm waiting for Colin."

At that moment the tall dark-haired boy walked toward her, sauntering along casually as if he were in no particular hurry. But his dark eyes were on no one but Meredith, sending her a message that made her heart race. She ignored her friends' pleas to join them. As if it were the most natural thing in the world, she marched straight down the hall and embraced him.

Every other Friday the cafeteria served fried chicken, and Meredith considered it the best meal the school served. The perfect meal to share with Colin. After they got their trays they looked for an empty table and found one near the door.

Meredith and Colin spent their lunch hour oblivious to the students around them. They didn't talk much, but Meredith felt they understood each other without words. Munching their fried chicken, they gazed into one another's eyes. Meredith felt peaceful and happy. When she and Colin had finished eating, Meredith noticed Liz and Patti heading for the moving tray return. Rising from deep inside her was an uncontrollable rage at their refusal to accept Colin. Who were they to tell her what to do?

"I have something to take care of. Do you mind?" she asked Colin sweetly.

"Not at all," he said. "Leave your tray. I'll take care of it for you."

Meredith darted into the crowded hallway

after the two girls. She could see her tall friend's copper-colored hair above most of the other heads.

"Patti. Liz," she called. "Wait up."

They stopped while she caught up. Liz's face was expressionless. She acted as though she'd been stopped by a total stranger. But Patti's eyes softened. She hoped Meredith wanted to make up after their silly argument. "What can we do for you?" Patti asked.

"Out here," Meredith said bluntly, motioning the girls toward a side door. "This will only take a minute and I want to be sure we talk in private."

The girls felt a blast of frigid air as Meredith opened the door.

"Meredith," Patti protested. "It's freezing out there, and we don't have our jackets."

"I need to talk to you," Meredith insisted, ignoring their pleas as she led them into the October air.

Patti and Liz hugged their books for warmth and they stood close together, facing the icy wind that whipped around the corner of the building. A gust sent leaves and papers scurrying across the pavement, yet Meredith appeared remarkably unaffected.

"What in the world is so important that

you have to drag us out here?" Liz demanded.

"I want to tell you something."

"What?" asked Patti impatiently. She hopped on one foot and then the other in a futile attempt to get warm.

"I never want either of you to speak to me again."

Meredith said the words slowly and deliberately and watched with satisfaction as she saw the stunned looks on her friends' faces. "You tried to turn me against Colin by calling him strange and weird, but it won't work. I care about him and he cares about me, and no so-called 'friends' are going to come between us."

Liz and Patti stared at her in disbelief, as if she were an alien from outer space. Silently they turned and walked back into the school, leaving Meredith alone in the cold wind.

She shivered, feeling a terrible chill run through her body that not even the bleak October weather could account for. How could she have dismissed her dear friends like that? She wanted to run after them, to tell them it was all a big mistake. But her legs seemed frozen in place.

Suddenly she thought of the note. YOUR FRIENDS ARE OUT TO BETRAY YOU. GET

THEM OUT OF YOUR LIFE. She'd done just what the message told her. She wanted to scream. YOU ARE IN MY POWER, the first note had said. Oh no, she thought as blackness enveloped her, I am!

Chapter Nine

Meredith had never dressed more carefully for a date. She was going to the movies with Colin. As she admired herself in the mirror, she could almost feel his eyes burn through her. She had chosen her new black sweater because she thought it made her look sophisticated and sexy. Colin would like that, she thought. This was going to be a special night, and she wanted to be sure she looked her best.

When she was satisfied with her outfit, Meredith went to her mirror and carefully applied her make-up. Then she styled her hair so it hid the snipped spot and fell softly over her shoulders. Everything had to be just right for Colin, and she stood back appraising herself until she was satisfied it was. He was so special, so very special.

Meredith wrapped her arms around herself and sighed. Closing her eyes for a moment she visualized his face. The image of his dark magnetic eyes made her feel as if she were diving into a bottomless pool, going deeper and deeper into the unfamiliar and yet closer and closer to where she wanted to be. How could Colin make her feel this way, she wondered, when not even Kit, whom she'd thought she loved with all her heart, could evoke such emotions within her?

Meredith wondered what Colin's adopted family was like. She'd looked up Dorn in the telephone book, but there was no listing.

Her thoughts were interrupted by the sound of the doorbell. She went to her bedroom door, opened it a crack, and listened as her father invited Colin inside. Her parents had been surprised when she'd announced her date with him, especially since she'd never mentioned him before.

Before going downstairs, Meredith made

a final check of her appearance in the full-length mirror hanging on her closet door. Through the door she heard her mother join Colin and her father. Then there was a strained silence, as if they had run out of things to say. Meredith had told her parents Colin was an orphan and sometimes had difficulty talking to people. This was such an important date. Why weren't they making more of an effort to make Colin feel at ease?

"Hello, everyone," she said as she entered the living room.

"Well, here she is," said her father, looking relieved she'd finally made her appearance.

"Hi, Colin." She smiled nervously, too shy to make conversation. "We might as well be going," she said at last. Colin nodded silently, and they headed for the door as Meredith said good night to her parents.

Colin led her to a sleek red Camaro parked at the curb. She got into the front seat and thought about Kit and his old brown station wagon. It was funny, she mused, how people's cars matched their personalities — reliable but boring Kit always picked her up in a station wagon, while moody and romantic Colin would whisk her away in a sports car.

Colin got into the car, closed the door, and turned to look at her. Without speaking, he held out his hand and pulled her close to him for a brief, hard kiss. It felt so right to Meredith, so natural. Her nervousness left her. Everything would be fine. They were safely enclosed in a world of their own.

Colin pulled away from the curb. Meredith looked at him with longing. He had never looked more handsome, more desirable; the shadowy evening light made him appear darkly mysterious.

Turning the corner, he left her neighborhood and eased into the Main Street traffic. He was quiet, but it was an exciting kind of quiet, like being powered by hot copper wires. Meredith felt herself wishing they were already at the movie theater, she was so anxious to show him off. Everyone went to the movies on Friday nights to see and be seen, and this would be her first public appearance with Colin. She was sure she'd be the envy of every girl there.

"Look at that crowd," she said as they turned another corner. The theater was now in sight, with its marquee proclaiming *The Curse of the Empty Coffin* in bright lights. A line of teenagers, two and three abreast, stretched from the box office all the way to the corner half a block away. Colin frowned and didn't answer, and Meredith began to wonder if he were wishing they'd gone somewhere more private.

She couldn't recall ever seeing him at a Friday night movie before.

He parked the car on the next block and said, "Why don't we wait until the line goes down?"

Meredith nodded, feeling as if she'd agree to anything he asked. They sat in the shadows and waited. The autumn evening was chilly, and she pulled her corduroy jacket tighter around her as they finally walked up the narrow sidewalk to the theater. She brightened, though, as she held Colin's hand under the clear, starry sky. She couldn't remember feeling happier, the terror of the past week a distant memory.

The number of people in line had dwindled to two or three by the time they reached the box office. There an elderly lady with short white hair and arthritic fingers pushed two tickets across the counter along with Colin's change. "Enjoy the picture," she called cheerily. Colin said nothing while Meredith nodded in response.

"Are you hungry?" asked Colin as they passed the crowded refreshment stand. Such a simple question, but Meredith didn't know if she was hungry or not.

"I'll get some popcorn," he said, and suddenly Meredith couldn't think of anything she'd like better.

Colin joined the line at the refreshment

stand as Meredith studied the groups of teenagers milling around the lobby. Suzy Gorham was standing with Dan Means near the glass case containing a poster for the next attraction. They had definitely seen her with Colin, although from the way they were staring at the poster, it was obvious they were trying to act as if they hadn't. Liz and Patti sauntered by with the Judson twins, Trish and Tammy, stopping their conversation abruptly when they saw her.

Liz was still miffed from the scene at lunch and walked right on by, but Patti stopped and smiled weakly. "Hi, Meredith. Are you here with Colin?"

Meredith was relieved that Patti was speaking to her. She wanted to explain that she hadn't meant what she said at lunch. Instead she heard herself say stiffly, "I thought I told you not to bother me anymore."

"But—"

"Patti, I said go away."

Meredith began to shake. Something's controlling me again, she thought desperately.

Suddenly Meredith felt someone looking at her. Kit. He was standing with a group of his track teammates and staring straight at her with his piercing blue eyes. She started toward him, but something held her back.

He came forward.

"Meredith, don't do it," he said.

"Don't do what?"

"Colin," he said, glancing in the direction of the tall boy. "He's no good for you."

Meredith felt something tearing her apart inside. She couldn't speak.

Kit sighed and lowered his eyes. "I'm sorry I asked for my ring back. I can't even remember what made us fight in the first place. All I know is that I still love you, I care about you so much, and the thought of you with this Dorn character gives me the shakes. I'd do anything to get you back." He seemed genuinely concerned and sorry.

Yes, Kit, yes, she thought. But she heard herself hiss, "It's too late, Kit." She turned abruptly, as if someone else were moving her limbs, and followed Colin down the dark aisle.

As she sat down next to Colin, her fears ebbed. She felt safe in his presence. Meredith scarcely tasted the popcorn. She barely saw the movie or heard the kids around her shrieking at the scary scenes. Her thoughts were concentrated on Colin, and Kit had disappeared from her mind. How thrilling it was to be with Colin!

When the movie ended, they waited to leave until after most of the other moviegoers had filed out of the theater. The lobby was quiet and the marquee dark. Outside the night was dark and pungent smelling and Meredith heard nothing but the steady rhythmic whisper of Colin's breathing. She knew everyone would be heading for either Ken's Pizza or the Pop Shoppe, but she was sure they would be the exception.

She was right. Colin drove straight to her house and parked the Camaro in the driveway. All the lights were out except for one in her own bedroom window. Her parents always left her desk lamp burning when they turned in early. She was alone with Colin in their own special world. His heavy masculine scent penetrated every pore of her being. Leaning back against the seat she looked up at Colin, but something in his expression startled her.

"What is it, Colin? Is something wrong?"

He made no sign that he'd heard her, and in the pale green glow of the dashboard lights his expression looked dark and almost sinister.

"Colin?" Meredith whispered, fear rising in her. "What's the matter with you?"

He took hold of her wrist with fingers of steel and pulled her toward him. "You really do love me, don't you Meredith? You're not just playing with me?"

She was afraid, but she couldn't resist

him.

"Of course I really love you." Meredith struggled to keep her voice steady. "I wouldn't joke about a thing like that. I'm not like that, believe me."

"Promise me you always will. *Always*."

"I promise. I will always love you." She felt empty when his grip loosened, but she couldn't draw her eyes away from his.

"I'm glad," he said. "Then you won't fail the test."

The test? Meredith wanted to ask just what this test was, but at that moment Colin pulled her up to him, kissing her hard on the mouth. After that it didn't matter. Nothing mattered but Colin.

The following morning Meredith was awakened by the sharp clanging of the telephone. Groggily she lifted the receiver. "Hello?" she mumbled.

"I think you should talk to Kit," Liz said, getting right to the point.

"Liz, what are you talking about?"

"We all went out for pizza last night after the movie and I think he wants to get back together with you."

Meredith was beginning to wake up. She remembered what Kit had said to her in the theater lobby. Liz could be right.

"But I thought you said I should never

take him back after the way he treated me," Meredith said, puzzled.

"Well, I've changed my mind. You've been acting strange ever since you took up with that Colin and I think Kit's much better for you."

Colin. With a thrill Meredith remembered their good night kiss. "Colin's the nicest boy I've ever met," she said defensively.

"But he's weird. And he was the one who found Missy."

"And it must have been an awful experience for him," Meredith said protectively.

"You'd better forget him," Liz said bluntly. "Now."

Forget about Colin? Never. "I bet you're just jealous because he's mine. But you can't have him!" she shouted, slamming down the phone.

For a long time Meredith lay there thinking about what her friend had said. Maybe Kit did want her back. She remembered how much she'd wanted to run to him last night. But then she thought of Colin and how urgently he'd wanted her to promise she'd love him always. She pondered her choices. She felt confused.

Chapter Ten

When Colin came to pick her up the next night, she met him at the door. Her parents had been uneasy about him and weren't pleased she was going out with him two nights in a row. She called good night and hurried out before they had the chance to come to the door.

Colin said nothing as he led her to the car. It wasn't until they had driven a few blocks and had eased into Main Street traffic that he finally spoke. "We aren't going to the movies in Denniston tonight," he said without taking his eyes off the road. "A James Bond picture is playing in Greyville. We'll see that," he said firmly.

"Okay," she said softly. "If that's what you want to do," she agreed, not wanting to cross him. She leaned back in the seat, telling herself she was lucky to be driving to the movies in a red Camaro with such a handsome boy. But her conversation with Liz tugged at the corners of her mind.

As they drove along the dark streets Meredith grew uneasy at Colin's silence. The night was dank and cool, the skies threatening rain, and she felt her sweater clinging to her skin. Except for telling her they were going to Greyville, he hadn't spoken to her at all. Meredith thought he was acting weird—and then scolded herself. No, she thought, not weird—that's the word Liz and Patti used to describe him. Colin was not weird, he was just different, the strong, silent type. It must be the weather that's making him feel so down. That wasn't weird—after all, hadn't she been depressed by the rain-filled clouds just the other night? She tried to convince herself that Colin would get over it.

"Speak to anyone today?" he asked after a while.

She gulped, thinking of Liz. "Only you . . . and my parents, of course." Then she added, "Oh, and Liz, early this morning."

"Liz doesn't like me," Colin said. He sounded sad and Meredith wanted to comfort him.

"It doesn't matter," she said, reaching for his hand. "I told her my loyalty is to you."

"Good," Colin said. He took her hand and grasped it so tightly Meredith could feel the blood draining from her fingers. He was so strong it almost frightened her. And so possessive. She looked at his determined profile and knew if she so much as looked at another boy he'd fly off the handle. That's probably why we're going to Greyville tonight, she thought. He couldn't stand to see her around anyone she knew.

There was little traffic on the highway and she stared at the road as it cut a dusky path through the dark countryside. There was no moon, and soon a light rain began to fall. Meredith shivered in the darkness and without thinking scratched the stubby hairs behind her ear. She was glad when the warm lights of Greyville finally came into view.

Colin parked the car in a narrow public lot across the street from the Greyville Cinema. The theater was a small, ancient single-story building set into a line of shabby store fronts that stretched for two blocks and made up the entire shopping district of the tiny town. The marquee read: *The Hound of the Baskervilles.*

"Colin," Meredith said, "it's not James Bond tonight."

"Yes it is," he said, unconcerned.

"But look at the sign."

"Trust me."

Colin grabbed her hand and pulled her across the street. He planted her in front of the rectangular glass case on the side of the theater and pointed to the sign. It read: SPECIAL PERFORMANCE — *For Your Eyes Only.*

"But how did you know?"

Colin did not answer. His eyes penetrated her soul and within a second Meredith had forgotten she'd even asked the question. His eyes were dark and commanding, willing her to look at him. How could she ever resist those eyes? she wondered as she gazed up at him. He always seemed to know when she had doubts about his love or when she was tempted to slip away from him. A shadow passed across Colin's face, making him look peculiar, like something out of a dream. Meredith felt the strength of his grip on her hand and shuddered.

Colin paid for the tickets and led the way into the theater, not bothering to stop at the refreshment stand this time. She thought perhaps he'd offer to go back for popcorn once they had found seats, but he didn't — and she was afraid to ask him to.

The interior of the theater was even shabbier than the front. The seats, once cushioned in plush dark-red velvet, were now threadbare from years of use, and the maroon curtain trimmed with tarnished gold braid that hung across the stage was limp and forlorn. In a few minutes the theater darkened, the curtain parted, and the movie began.

At first Meredith was engrossed in the film but gradually she became aware of a strange sensation. She'd never been to this theater before, yet something about it was familiar. Involuntarily she shivered, finding little relief in Colin's caress. Something was nagging at the back of her mind. She tried to figure out why the theater seemed so familiar, but a sudden sharp pain filled her head. When she looked up, she saw Colin staring at her. She was unable to decipher the message he was sending, but she could tell he was troubled by something. He reached for her hand roughly and gripped it hard.

The ride home was quiet. Meredith was confused by something she couldn't put her finger on. Colin pulled the Camaro into her driveway and turned off the ignition. He pulled her close to him and Meredith felt the strength of his arms around her.

"You'll always love me, won't you?" Colin's words were more of a command than a question. Without waiting for an answer he placed his lips on hers, and Meredith was lost in the depths of his kiss.

She lay awake for a long time thinking about Colin. She realized she had been pining for a stranger, a mystery man who would swoop into her life to fill the empty void left by Kit's betrayal. Colin. She really didn't know much about him, what he was interested in, what he was going to do after high school, what he liked or who his friends were—all the silly, unimportant things people shared with each other when they went together. He had said he wanted to spend his time with her; he was elated she'd dropped out of the Student Council race so she could be with him. And . . . he told her over and over with his eyes that he loved her. His eyes, she thought with a sigh. His beautiful, terrible eyes. He could look inside her mind with those eyes and penetrate the deepest part of her soul.

But what was that lingering sensation of fear that hovered over her thoughts? She had felt something wasn't quite right, sitting with him in that desolate, oddly familiar theater. She thought of Liz's warning to forget the dark-haired boy and shivered at the memory of his strong arms around her. Why did she sense such anger and bitterness in those dark brooding eyes? Why did she feel as if something terrible was about to explode inside him?

Chapter Eleven

Sunday morning Meredith awoke stiff and groggy from a night of tossing and turning, of waking and dozing, but always with Colin in the back of her mind. Only for a short time was she able to forget him during church services. But once she came home he dominated her thoughts again.

"It's a gorgeous day," her mother said as the two of them sat on stools at the kitchen counter eating lunch. "Why don't you get together with Liz or Patti? I'm sure you girls could find something interesting to do."

Meredith nibbled at her chicken salad and gazed out the kitchen window at her father raking leaves in the back yard. She wanted to be alone to sort out her thoughts about Colin. "Liz and Patti are busy today," she lied.

"Both of them?" Her mother raised an eyebrow in surprise.

"Uh, huh," said Meredith as she stuffed her face with a huge forkful of food. She did it purposely, even though it nearly made her sick to her stomach.

"You seem so blue today. Your eyes look a little tired."

Meredith winced at the mention of eyes.

"Didn't things go well on your date last night? I've wanted to ask you about Colin. He seemed rather peculiar to me."

"There's nothing wrong with Colin," Meredith said a little uncertainly.

"Are you sure you're all right, dear? You've seemed edgy all week."

"I'm fine, Mom. Everyone gets into bad moods sometimes. It'll pass. It's nothing."

Her mother shrugged. "Didn't mean to pry." She paused and then said, "If you'd like to get out of the house for a while, I have an errand that needs running. How about it?"

"Okay," said Meredith. It would do her

good to get out. She could be by herself and figure things out.

Meredith rinsed their plates and glasses and put them into the dishwasher while her mother went upstairs for the car keys. "I'd like you to go to Killinger's Market and pick up the leg of lamb I ordered. I think this will be enough to cover it," her mother said, handing Meredith two ten-dollar bills along with the keys. "Drive around awhile or stop at the Pop Shoppe if you want."

"Thanks, Mother, see you later." Meredith pulled her pile-lined corduroy jacket from a hanger, fished around in the hat and glove box on the closet floor for her mittens, and hurried out of the house. The cold air was invigorating, and she breathed a sigh of relief as she backed her mother's yellow compact car out of the driveway.

She decided Claymore Park would be a good place to sit and think. It was her favorite spot and it would be quiet today. Ernest Claymore had been one of the founding fathers of Denniston. He had built the park complete with a small band shell where the town band still gave concerts on Thursday evenings during the summer. At one end of the park was a lovely lake surrounded by a grove of majestic white pine trees. Meredith always found the lake a relaxing place to visit. That's where she'd go to think.

Meredith drove through the tall wrought-iron gate at the park's entrance and meandered along the winding narrow road to the lake. When she reached her destination, she switched off the ignition and let the silence fill her ears.

Leaning back in the seat, she sighed, picturing Colin and his dark magnetic eyes. She'd never experienced such excitement with a boy. He was much more fascinating than Kit.

Kit. Her thoughts swung toward him. She smiled, thinking of all the happy summer afternoons they'd spent swimming in this very lake. He might not be as exciting as Colin, but they'd known each other for so long, and he'd always been so reliable. Until their fight before the assembly, that is. Meredith felt small and vulnerable as she remembered how his words had hurt her. Could he really want her back? On the phone Liz had sounded so sure he did.

Meredith tried to recall exactly what her friend had said, and then she remembered Liz's comment about how strange Meredith had been acting lately. Yes, the week had been dreadful, she thought, closing her eyes. Suddenly, the blood-red letters of the three mysterious notes flashed through her mind, only to be replaced by the gleaming ruby eyes from her dreams. She opened her eyes quickly and gazed at the peaceful scene before her. As she stared at the still surface of the lake, she thought of the wonderful calm feeling that enveloped her in Colin's presence. Being with him had been the only good thing about the past week. She sighed, thinking of his kisses. Suddenly a fierce longing rose inside her. She wanted nothing more than to be with Colin.

Missing him terribly, Meredith stared sadly off into the trees. Her eyes caught sight of two dark figures, a boy and a girl, strolling along the cobblestone path that led from the parking lot, across a wide expanse of grass, and all the way to the band shell. They seemed to be moving slowly, as in a dream. But as they came closer Meredith could begin to make out their forms. It was Colin—and beside him, Liz.

Meredith gasped. She couldn't believe her eyes. What on earth could the two of them be doing together? Liz had acted as though she despised Colin, and it was impossible to think he liked her much better.

Afraid they'd see her, Meredith crouched low in the seat and peered out at them through the steering wheel. It was Liz and Colin all right. They were deep in conversation, their faces close together as they walked.

Of all the two-faced things to do, thought

Meredith, enraged. No wonder Liz wanted me to make up with Kit. She wanted Colin for herself!

She stared at them in disbelief. They were walking slowly in spite of the unseasonably chilly weather. Then Meredith saw Colin put his arm around Liz and pull her tightly against him. Hot sparks of jealousy exploded inside Meredith and she swung open the car door, determined to confront her betrayers. But as she ran down the path toward them, she stumbled and looked to see what she'd tripped on. Cobblestones. Meredith gasped. This was the path she'd seen in her dreams.

Dizzy with fear, she shut her eyes for a moment and saw those burning ruby beads at the end of the cobblestone path, the twin beams in her dreams. She opened her eyes in terror and, seeing Colin steering Liz around the lake, sank to the ground in tears. The path swam before her eyes and then she sat up with a start. At last she knew who the figure was who called her in the dreams, commanding her to obey. It was Colin!

Meredith felt a white-hot pain burn through her. Colin had been in her dreams. Colin had sent her the notes. Meredith blinked quickly, unsure now if she was awake or dreaming. The fiery sensation gave way to a gripping chill and her limbs froze. It was true. Colin could read her mind and send her messages with his dark, brooding eyes. She agreed to whatever he suggested as if she were a robot with no will of her own. Colin could do things that no one else could do. She really was in his power, as surely as if she dangled from puppet strings he held in his hands.

How could she have been so blind? Why had she ignored the warnings she'd gotten from her friends? Then she remembered the second note and its ominous admonition not to listen to them. Colin had wanted her not to listen, so she hadn't. It was as simple as that.

I've got to resist him, she thought desperately. I've got to get away from here! Scrambling back to the car, Meredith shot away from the curb, burning patches of rubber behind her. She left the park by the back gate and drove through town barely noticing the traffic lights. She had to piece things together, but her thoughts tumbled through her mind, colliding with each other and going off like firecrackers.

I must be going crazy, she thought wildly. I must be mad! Meredith pulled off the road and stopped, trying to slow her heart's frantic beating. But she felt even more out of control when she looked around and realized she'd left Denniston and had been driving along the highway to Greyville — the same road she and Colin had traveled the night before. She wanted to scream, but couldn't. Was Colin controlling her even now?

Meredith stopped the car and rested her arms against the steering wheel, laid her head down, and cried. What was she going to do? She couldn't sort it out alone. Her mind was whirling too fast. She couldn't concentrate. I have to talk to someone, she thought. But who?

Her parents? Her father would probably lock her in her room and call the hospital, refusing to believe such a wild story could be true. I'll call Patti, she thought. After all, Patti had tried to make up with her at the movie theater after that awful scene at lunch. Then Meredith remembered how rude she'd been to her friend at the theater. If only Patti would forgive her now and listen to her story.

Meredith waited for the traffic to clear and then pulled onto the highway again, circling around and heading back toward Denniston. She felt a little better now that she had decided on a course of action. She could stop by Patti's house. Her thoughts darted. No, it would be better to call first. She had a big apology to make and looking

Patti in the eye would be awfully hard. She'd call from home. Home, she thought, savoring the sound of the word.

Meredith sped toward her house. It wasn't until she was two blocks from home that she remembered the meat her mother had asked her to pick up. How will I ever be able to figure things out if I can't even remember a stupid leg of lamb? Hysteria mounted inside Meredith as she circled back to the meat market. She whisked into the parking lot behind the store and hurried in for her purchase. The butcher gave the pale, wide-eyed girl a questioning look as he handed her the change. Oh, no, thought Meredith, if I'm not careful, everyone will think I'm going crazy. She gasped. I am going crazy!

She took deep breaths as she pulled into her driveway and walked into the kitchen. Flashing her mother a weak smile, Meredith put the package of meat and a few crumpled bills on the counter.

"Here you are, Mother. I even brought change." She tried to sound normal.

"Thanks, dear." Meg Turner gave her daughter a concerned look. "Are you feeling better after your drive?"

"Sure," Meredith lied. "I went to Claymore Park. It was sort of nice to be by myself."

Her mother looked at her, frowning. "I'm

glad it did you some good to get out of the house. But you know I'm here if you ever need to talk."

"Thanks, Mom." Meredith turned away quickly. If only she could confide in her mother this time. But she had seen the strange look her mother gave her. Her parents would have her sent away if they heard her crazy tale.

"I'll be helping your father finish trimming the roses in the back yard," her mother called out as Meredith ran upstairs.

Meredith listened for the back door to close and picked up the phone. Patti's got to understand, she prayed silently as she dialed the number. It rang once, twice, three times.

"Hello?" came a voice on the other end of the line.

"Oh, Mrs. Hayden," Meredith breathed. "Is Patti there?"

"No, she's not. She's visiting her grandmother in Hadley and won't be home until late tonight. Can you talk to her at school tomorrow?"

Meredith caught her breath. "Okay," she said, panic tightening her throat.

Meredith heard a few clicks followed by the atonal hum of the disconnect signal. She stared at the lifeless telephone for a few moments, then slammed down the receiver and began to weep. I've got to tell someone what's going on, she thought desperately. I've got to talk to somebody *now*. But who?

Missy would understand. But Missy was dead. The horrible fact took Meredith's breath away, and dreadful visions flooded her mind. Stark negative images set against shadowless landscapes. Missy lying lifeless in Claymore Lake. Meredith hurrying toward a misty figure along a cobblestone path. Meredith gasped. Colin had found Missy. And Colin was the figure in her dream. Maybe he'll come after me next, she nearly screamed. Meredith could see Colin staring down at her, commanding her with his eyes, his power growing inside her, possessing her very soul. The eyes grew larger and larger, turning from black to red. Meredith felt the room spinning and she was swallowed by a black terror.

When she came to, Meredith was drenched in a cold sweat. "I've got to talk to someone before I go crazy," she said aloud. The sound of her own voice made her feel a little calmer. Kit, she thought. Kit would know what to do.

The telephone receiver felt heavy in her hand as she picked it up. What was his number? She had called it so many times it should be easy to remember. This is silly, she thought. Now what is it? 786. That much she could recall, but what came after that? A 4? Or was it a 3? She closed her eyes, trying to picture the number, but digits bounced around in her mind's eye like Mexican jumping beans. 9 ... 1 ... 7 ... 4 ... 2. 786, she thought stubbornly. Now come on, what comes next? It was an 0 ... and then a 4. No! It was a 4 ... and then an 0 ... and then a 3 ... and a 9. But what was the first part?

She closed her eyes again. Take it easy, she told herself, you know you know it. Try it one more time. 786-4039. Finally.

She reached for the dial with her right hand, but her index finger would not move. She jabbed at the dial over and over again with her limp hand, but she could not make her finger fit into it. "What's wrong?" she screamed. "What's wrong with me?"

Meredith sank to the floor, letting the receiver dangle from its cord and bump softly against the wall. "I *am* going crazy," she whispered. "It's happening. I'm in Colin's power." She wanted to cry but the tears were stuck in her eyes. She was oblivious to everything except the sharp bleep of the telephone telling her the receiver was off the hook.

She was still standing by the telephone a little while later, when she heard sounds at the back door. Her parents had finished their yard work and were coming in.

Meredith raced downstairs to the kitchen. I have to tell them, she thought. No matter what they think, I have to tell them everything.

"What's wrong dear?" her mother asked, hurrying to her. "Are you all right?"

Her father frowned and moved closer. "What is it, sweetheart?"

Meredith looked up at them through tear-filled eyes. She had to get the words out before it was too late. "I'm scared," she began. "He's coming for me . . ." She tried to go on, but her lips refused to move and no sound came out except for a low moan.

Mrs. Turner hugged her daughter. "No, honey. There's nothing to worry about. They caught that Sondergard fellow this afternoon. He confessed to the Stevens murder."

Meredith shook her head, trying to get her mother to understand there was more than one evil spirit lurking in the town. She tried again and again, willing herself to speak, as convulsive sobs shook her body. She could feel the words inside her mouth. She could taste their bitterness, feel their scorching heat. They were growing larger, filling her mouth, threatening to choke her, and though she struggled to breathe around them she could not force them out. With one last effort, she lunged forward and collapsed into her father's arms.

She felt him lift her and gently carry her to her room. Her mother turned down the covers, pulled off her shoes, and tucked her in as if she were a helpless baby. Her eyes were open and she could hear everything that was going on, and yet she could not speak.

"Let's let her rest for a while," her mother said. "If she isn't feeling better by dinner time, we'll call Dr. Post."

They tiptoed out and closed the door, leaving her alone as the duskiness of late afternoon settled in her room. She lay there locked in fear, knowing she was trapped inside a body that refused to respond to her commands. She had tried to call Kit, but could not dial the number. She had tried to talk to her parents, but the words would not come through her lips. There was nothing she could do, no one she could turn to for help. Colin wouldn't let her.

She tried to stop thinking of him, but she couldn't banish the vision of his dark, sinister eyes from her mind. Maybe I should concentrate on something else, she thought. She focused all her thoughts on Kit, on that smile she loved so much. Somehow she knew if she could tell Kit she was in trouble, he would help. Kit would have an answer.

Thinking of Kit, Meredith felt her muscles relax. Exhausted, she finally drifted off to sleep, but even in her subconscious state she could find little peace. Again she returned to that fog-enshrouded place, looking into the deep, dark lake that had been so inviting in her earlier dream. Only this time someone was lying there, a body beckoning to her. Missy Price. On her face was a serene smile, and her eyes were focused upward. "Meredith," she called plaintively. "Meredith don't fail the test. The real test. You have the power . . ."

Drenched in sweat, Meredith awoke from the dream with a start. The dream had been a warning, she knew, a warning to escape from Colin's grasp. Could she indeed unlock herself from his power—or was it already too late? she wondered as she looked around the room, the late afternoon shadows rising around it, standing somberly like mourners at a wake.

The funeral. Missy's funeral was the next morning, and Meredith had a premonition she'd find the answer there. She fell into a deep sleep, a sleep that lasted till the cold hours of dawn.

Chapter Twelve

Meredith rose early. Missy's funeral would be getting under way at nine, and she wanted to make sure she had plenty of time to get ready. She felt her spirits rise a little when she saw the rain pummeling the sidewalk and street outside her window. Someone had once told her it always rained on the funerals of good people, and Meredith took it as a sign that her premonition about Missy's warning was correct.

As she dressed, the pains began. They were sharp, piercing attacks in the center of her head that in normal times would most likely have driven her right back into bed. But she willed herself to bear them. Nothing was going to stop her from going to the funeral. Nothing short of death.

She crept out of the house early, snatching her mother's car keys from the latch by the door where she always hung them.

Arriving at the large white funeral home, Meredith parked the car on the side street and slipped in through the side door. The pain in her head was so strong now she hardly noticed that the downpour had soaked her clothes or that the humidity in the air had transformed her hair into a mass of disconnected frizzy tendrils. All she knew was she had to go inside.

Hampered by another painful attack, Meredith slowly crept down the narrow gray-carpeted hallway until she came to a door with the sign MISSY PRICE tacked onto it with black plastic letters. Inside, the room was dominated by the flower-strewn casket made of black oak with heavy brass handles. And lying there on a bed of red satin was Missy. Obscuring her from Meredith's view were a sad-eyed man and woman in their early forties. Missy's parents.

Meredith took her place in the line of people waiting to pay their last respects. A few minutes later she saw Kit arrive and felt her heart race wildly. He passed by her silently, casting her a strange, puzzled expression. She tried to stop him to explain everything, but the pain was so strong she could hardly stand up, let alone speak. Yet she managed one plaintive look in his direction. Meredith felt he must have misunderstood its meaning, however, since he merely shook his head and moved on. Patti was there too, up at the front of the line, but she didn't see Meredith, and Meredith made no effort to approach her. She didn't have the strength.

As she reached the front of the line Meredith could overhear Missy's parents deep in conversation with another couple. "We'll never understand," Mr. Price was saying. "Missy was such a good student, but in her note she said she failed the test."

Oh, my God, Meredith cried silently as she remembered her latest dream. Her dear dead friend really must have been trying to communicate with her last night. Meredith walked slowly toward the coffin and then she saw it. The undertaker had tried to conceal it, but right under Missy's ear — her left ear — was a stubbly patch where a lock of her hair had been shorn. It was all true!

Then just as suddenly as it had begun, the pain in her head stopped. Without knowing why, Meredith ran out of the room and into the rain-soaked street. All of a sudden she couldn't remember why she was standing outside this funeral home under the rain. She couldn't remember why she wasn't in school on this Monday morning.

A nagging thought hung just out of reach in her mind. What was it? She frowned, trying to pull it forward, but as quickly as it had come it was gone again, like the shadow of a bird in flight.

Suddenly a blissful calm came over her. She knew only that she had to get to Claymore Park. Colin would be waiting for her there. Colin would explain everything. She could hear him calling her name now as her feet led her toward the car. She had to hurry. He had something planned for her, something very special.

She felt slightly disoriented and the streets seemed oddly unfamiliar. But she drove quickly, as if someone were leading her along the route. A right hand turn, a left, and finally she recognized a landmark, Ken's Pizza, where she had spent so much time with Kit.

With the thought of Kit came a sudden fear, a gripping terror that made her tremble. Why was Kit in her mind? Why was she so afraid? What was it she could not recall? She swerved, barely missing an oncoming car as she pushed the accelerator toward the floor. Colin would have the answer.

Claymore Park was just ahead now, standing out against the twinkle of lights shining against the dark skies of the storm. At the entryway she swung through the massive iron gate, switched on her headlights and proceeded slowly along the narrow road. It was darker in the park where the evergreen trees met overhead, almost as dark as night. Even the oak trees, with their bare branches skeletonlike in their starkness, covered the immediate horizon, forming a weblike canopy overhead through which the rain continued to fall.

Claymore Lake appeared through the trees. She stared at its surface, smooth and calm now that the rain had stopped. The pull was even stronger now. Irresistible. Colin was calling to her and she had to meet him.

Driving into the parking lot, she stopped and switched off both the engine and the lights. She studied the frigid landscape around her, but nothing moved. Where was Colin? She had to hurry. He was waiting.

As soon as she stepped onto the cobblestone path, she felt better. She had been here before. She peered into the darkness and saw a figure at the end of the path. Her pulse quickened. It was him. He was waiting for her, beckoning to her just as she had known he would. Meredith wanted nothing but to be with the figure in the distance. She hurried along the cobblestones until the path ended and she stood ankle-deep in cold wet grass. She shivered. A sharp prick of fear disturbed her ecstasy. Suddenly she realized this was the landscape of her dream.

The figure was walking slowly toward her now, the mist covering his face. With each step he took, Meredith felt fear grip her tighter. When he had almost reached Meredith his face emerged through the haze. Colin's gleaming black eyes flashed at her. Her blood ran cold as the dark face she feared leered over her. She felt his hand close over her mouth.

"I'm glad you got here so quickly, Meredith," hissed Colin. Then, laughing evilly, he looked into her eyes. "Don't try to run. You can't. YOU ARE IN MY POWER."

Chapter Thirteen

"YOU ARE IN MY POWER." The terrible words echoed through the dreary park.

Colin's eyes held Meredith's, glowing strangely, like burning embers of evil. Meredith felt doomed.

"Does anyone know you're here?" he asked.

She felt his grip loosen, but still she scarcely dared to breathe. "No," she said almost inaudibly, regretting the truth of the word. She was alone and helpless against his strength.

Colin took her arm roughly. "Let's go for a walk," he said.

Meredith nodded sadly as they tramped across the dark grass toward the pond. If only I could break away from him, she thought desperately. But her arm ached within his terrible grip, and she feared escape was impossible.

"Don't be afraid of me, Meredith."

"I'm not afraid," Meredith lied.

"Good. Because I know you have reason to be."

"What do you mean?"

"I know you went to Missy's funeral."

At the mention of her dead friend, Meredith gasped. Was she his next victim?

"And you saw the mark," Colin continued.

"The missing hair? Yes." Meredith paused. "You killed Missy, didn't you?"

"I had to. She gave me no choice."

"Why?" Meredith cried. "She was sweet and would never hurt a soul. Why did you have to kill her?"

The two of them were approaching a bench and Colin motioned for Meredith to stop. After they were seated, he turned to face her. "I don't have to tell you, but since it makes no difference now, I'll explain. You see, last year I got the mark too. One day I walked far into the woods in back of our house. I came across a big underground pit. It looked old and I decided to go exploring. The pit opened up into this big chamber. It was too dark to see what was inside and I was about to climb out, when it started to rain. I didn't want to get wet so I stayed there and soon fell asleep.

"I had a dream in which three old women led me down a long road lit by two fiery beams. From the end of the road I heard a voice calling my name and telling me that I had the chance to receive a very special gift. I would be given the power to control other people with my thoughts—on one condition. I had to pledge my soul to the being who called out to me. If I made that vow, I would one day be able to make anyone do whatever I wished. When I woke up, I was terrified and tried to convince myself that my imagination had just been playing tricks on me. But when I got home I realized a lock of my hair was missing, and I knew the dream had been real.

"I was drawn back to the secret underground chamber the next day. I pledged my soul. The voice told me that if I made daily visits to the cave to show my devotion, my mental powers would eventually develop into a powerful tool that could control anyone on earth." He paused. "And I was given this ring."

A chill ran down Meredith's spine as she looked down at his finger. There on his hand was a ring with two finely faceted rubies that gleamed just like the eyes in her dream.

"My old school was a good place to try out my power," Colin continued. "I had never been happy there because no one seemed to have the time to befriend a quiet boy like me. Once I received this ring, if someone called me a sissy I could make him fall on his face. When a teacher began to criticize me I was able to make her forget and compliment me instead. My power grew and grew. But although I could make everyone respect me, I couldn't force them to be my friends.

"Finally my parents grew annoyed with my daily trips to the cave. My mother complained that I didn't help enough around the house and my father insisted I was neglecting my homework. So they forbade me to go into the woods. I was furious! I was so mad I wished they were dead. If I didn't visit the secret chamber each day, I was afraid I would lose my gift. And I didn't yet have as much power as I wanted—I didn't have the power to make others love me."

As he said the word "love," Colin looked deeply into Meredith's eyes. His dark gaze gripped her and her body froze.

"I ran out of the house and into the woods. When I told the fiery-eyed being what had happened, he said I had proven my devotion and that I didn't need to return to him.

"The next morning my parents died on their way to work. The police said it was a car accident, but I knew it was because of my wish the night before. That's when I came to Denniston."

Meredith grew chillier as Colin revealed his story. He had power over life and death, she realized, thinking of Missy.

"When I came to school here, I found it was the same old thing. No one had time for a newcomer. Nobody, that is, except for your friend Missy. She saw me sitting alone on the school steps two weeks ago and stopped to talk."

"But I never saw you with her," Meredith protested weakly.

"I never let you. I wanted her all to myself."

"So why did you kill her?"

"I wanted her to love me, to join me in my power forever. So I took a lock of her hair and asked her to pledge herself to me forever. But she resisted. She failed the test. By then she knew too much and I had no choice but to kill her."

Meredith touched the stubby hairs behind her left ear and gasped. "And what about me?" She feared the answer, her heart pounding in her chest like a lead ball against a hollow drum as she waited for his response.

"When Missy wouldn't love me I turned to you because you were one of her friends."

"But why did you choose me?" she said hysterically. "Why not Patti or Liz?"

"You and Missy looked almost like sisters. And I'd seen you arguing with Kit earlier the day Missy betrayed me. You looked vulnerable and hurt and I thought you might be willing to give me the love she refused. And besides, the election intrigued me. At first I thought that if you won the election, you might lead the entire school to me."

Meredith thought of her blackout during the assembly and shivered.

"Yes," said Colin, reading her thoughts. "I was the one who gave you the words for your speech. But then I realized that if you won the election you would be spending a lot of time with Kit on Student Council, and I was afraid you'd want to go back to him. So I made you drop out of the election."

It was all too much for Meredith. Colin really had been controlling her. Kit, she thought desperately, trying to concentrate her thoughts on the one person she felt might be able to save her. Kit, where are you?

Colin sensed that she was thinking of his rival, and he tightened his grip on her arm. "Will you come with me, Meredith, join in my power and be mine forever? Or are you going to be like Missy?"

A scream rose in Meredith's throat as she thought of what Colin had done to Missy.

"If you know what's good for you, you won't fail this test."

Meredith trembled as she heard his words. She remembered the warning Missy had sent her in the dream last night. She had to resist him. But Colin was holding her tightly and she began to cry. "But Colin, don't you see? It's no good this way. I do love you, but I'm so frightened."

"But do you love me enough to be mine forever? You've doubted me, Meredith. You doubted me when we went to the movies in Greyville. You doubted me yesterday when you wanted to talk to Patti and your parents. And you doubted me when you tried to call Kit," he said in a sinister voice, his eyes glowing with hate at the thought of his rival.

Kit, oh, Kit, where are you? she thought desperately. She remembered the blond-haired boy's smile, the look in his eyes when he'd tell her he loved her. His love for her was pure and gentle, not like Colin's — Colin wanted to possess her, to bend her will to his own. The thought of Kit made her heart leap hopefully. She knew she had to try to resist Colin's evil power. If only she could talk him out of this.

"I loved you, Colin. Really I did. But I was afraid that you didn't love me when I saw you walking around the lake yesterday with Liz —" She stopped short, panic making her blood race through her veins. "Colin, what did you do to Liz?"

He pulled her roughly to her feet and steered her toward the lake. Meredith looked at him in terror and saw the evil in his eyes deepen. His pupils turned fiery red and her blood turned to ice.

"Liz was worried about you," he said with an evil laugh. "She never liked me. She thought you'd been acting strangely ever since you started spending time with me. So she confronted me and told me to leave you alone. But she didn't understand who she was up against." His burning eyes flashed at Meredith. "I made her come down here."

"Why did you let me see the two of you?"

"I didn't," Colin admitted. "It was a mistake. You see, my power only works on one person at a time. I had to concentrate all my thoughts on making Liz do what I wanted her to do. It wasn't until later I realized you'd decided on your own to come to the park."

"Then what happened?" Meredith's heart sank as she waited for him to tell her the dreadful truth.

Colin's eyes grew larger and brighter, and he looked like an animal the likes of which Meredith had never imagined.

"I convinced her to dive into the lake the same way I convinced Missy." He pulled a sheet of paper from his pocket and shoved it in front of Meredith's face. Liz's last words. Words she was forced to write by this demon.

Meredith's heart stopped. She screamed, but Colin quickly forced his hand over her mouth. Liz was dead. Colin had used his terrible power on poor Liz—the only person who tried to help her. He had forced Liz to commit suicide.

Meredith struggled, kicking and flailing at him wildly. The lake was no more than a few feet away, and Colin laughed savagely as he dragged her toward it.

He paused at the water's edge and the smile drained from his face. "Now are you with me, Meredith? Are you ready to join me?"

"Never!" she shouted.

"I can't make you love me, but I can make you die if you don't," he said viciously. He stared into her eyes intently. "It looks like I'll have to convince you to go for a swim too."

"No!" cried Meredith her voice rasping in pure terror. "No, Colin, no!"

Still staring at her with those terrible eyes, he let go of her. I've got to run away, Meredith thought. But her legs felt like pillars of stone. "No," she moaned. She had to resist. Kit, she thought. Silently she repeated his name over and over, trying to hold the image of his face in her mind.

Colin's face was the face of death. "It won't work, Meredith. You can't resist me. In a moment you're going to walk into the lake and dive into its depths. You're going to want to swim to the bottom of it."

Meredith tried to concentrate on Kit, to remember his face and his blond hair. But she was suddenly so tired her knees buckled slightly. She found herself taking tiny steps toward the water.

"That's right, Meredith. Take another step. It's a lovely day for a swim. Come on. One more step now."

Meredith felt her concentration ebbing. She could barely remember what had happened a minute earlier. Suddenly she felt as if she were wrapped in the delicious warmth of an August evening. She heard the water slosh around her feet as walked into the lake. Why, it's beautiful weather for a swim, she thought.

Then out of the corner of her eye she saw a dark, damp mass that had washed up on shore. It was Liz's body!

Just then a bright light flashed through the dark pines, and the wail of a car horn honking wildly startled Colin, momentarily breaking his concentration. Meredith tried to run, but Colin pushed her into the lake with terrible force. "You're not getting away from me," he screamed, eyes ablaze.

The cold water cleared her brain a little. Surfacing, Meredith gasped for air and looked over her shoulder. Colin was about to jump in after her.

Meredith took a deep breath and swam with all her might, reaching the shore partway around the lake before Colin could catch up with her.

Shedding her sodden jacket, she ran as fast as she could toward the pines, screaming at the top of her lungs for help. She entered the dark woods, now almost completely enveloped in fog. She didn't know where she was headed, but an instinct for survival gave her a kind of inner radar, and she sidestepped trees and bushes as if she were being guided by a power even greater than Colin's. But try as she could, the echo of his footsteps followed her like a curse. If only I can make it through the fog, she thought desperately.

"You'll never escape." Colin's voice sounded very close, as if he'd catch up to her any minute.

Meredith scrambled up the densely wooded incline, gasping for breath. Suddenly the mist cleared and Meredith could see where she was—at the top of Claymore Peak, the highest point in the town. The precipice reached its apex not far from where she stood and on the other side, she knew, there was a hundred-foot drop to a narrow rivulet that flowed toward Hadley. She panicked. Where could she go from here?

She paused for a second, breathing heavily, and glanced back over her shoulder. There was Colin—only ten feet away. His eyes flashed at her and as she started to run again, his piercing glare made her stumble over a dead tree branch that had been knocked down by the wind.

Before she could regain her footing Colin reached her. He leaned over her, taking a pair of shiny silver scissors from his jacket pocket. Meredith screamed.

"I told you it was impossible to escape from me," he cried, the words like icy daggers piercing Meredith's heart. He held the sharp instrument over his head.

"Colin, no! Please, please don't hurt me!"

"I wanted you to worship me. But you wouldn't," he hissed, opening the scissors and slowly lowering a razor-sharp blade to her neck.

Meredith winced as she felt the cold metal on her skin. Slowly and deliberately he drew the blade across her neck, and Meredith felt a thin line of pain at the base of her skull. "Colin —" she gasped, writhing. She realized she would die.

He laughed eerily. "Don't worry, it's only a flesh wound. I wanted to see you squirm, to suffer for refusing me." His eyes bored deep into her soul, as if that was all he needed to keep her in place. He was smiling maniacally.

"Colin, don't —" she screamed.

"Okay, Meredith, I'll put you out of your misery now." Colin raised his arm, poising the scissors above her head.

Meredith closed her eyes in terror just as a hand grabbed Colin's arm from behind. She fell back weakly as her unidentified savior pulled Colin away from her, wrestling with him for the weapon. She heard something fall to the ground inches away from her head as the two struggled in the murky darkness.

Suddenly, Colin pushed the other person

to the ground and ran wildly to the top of Claymore Peak. Hearing the sound of his retreat, Meredith opened her eyes just in time to see him turn back and shout, "You'll never find me, never!" before he leaped off the rocky precipice.

Chapter Fourteen

"Oh, Kit," Meredith sobbed as she fell into his arms. "It's so awful. He tried to kill me. And Liz. Her body's down at the lake."

Kit put a handkerchief around Meredith's neck to stop the bleeding wound. Then he held her tight, rocking her gently and stroking her hair as she cried. Shaken by convulsive sobs, she let her tears flow on and on until she was exhausted. She lay there in his arms.

"You're okay now," Kit whispered. "Everything's going to be all right. Colin's dead."

"But he killed Missy and Liz," she whimpered, tears welling up in her eyes again. "Thank goodness you found me in time." She looked up at him in confusion. "How did you know I was here? How did you know about Colin?"

"Patti figured it out." Meredith turned and realized for the first time that Patti was standing there, huffing heavily from the run up the hill. She looked at her friend, who was crying softly.

"I tried to call you back last night when I got home from my grandmother's, but your parents said you were asleep," said Patti. "My mother said you sounded sort of strange on the phone, and you'd been acting so odd all week. I got worried. So I tried to call Liz to see if she'd heard from you. But she wasn't there and when she didn't turn up at the funeral this morning, I got scared—" She stopped, out of breath.

"We saw you run out of the funeral," Kit put in. "And when Patti told me about Liz, I was afraid something might happen to you too. I remembered that they'd found Missy here and figured it was the first place we should look for you."

"Thank God you're safe," Patti said.

Kit nodded, hugging Meredith close to

143

him.

Slowly Meredith explained to them what had happened, about her strange overwhelming urge to come to Claymore Park and about what Colin had done to Liz. She trembled as she told them how his power had almost forced her to take her own life. She could feel tears welling up in her eyes again.

"You're safe now," Kit said, holding her close. "I'll never let you go again. Don't think about anything else right now."

Kit's arms felt good around her. She knew without a doubt that this was where she belonged. Kit was the one she really loved, and now she was certain he loved her, too.

"I guess we'll have to go to the police and tell them about Liz and where to find Colin's body." She sighed.

Meredith closed her eyes for a moment and saw Colin's strange, haunting eyes before her. In that instant she realized the terrible memory of him would stay with her forever.

Several hours later, Meredith received a call from the Denniston police asking her to go down to the station. Kit had taken her home to bandage her wound and rest while he went to tell the police what had happened.

Still shaken, but feeling calmer than she had for days, Meredith walked into the station and Kit rushed to her side. She saw his tender smile and was thankful for the love which, she realized, had saved her life.

"We're sorry we had to ask you to come down here," the officer said. "But since you were the last person to see Colin Dorn alive, we need you to identify these items we found in the creek below Claymore Peak." He spread some damp clothes across the desk. They were the black pants and jacket Colin had worn just a few hours earlier.

"Yes, those are his," Meredith said, looking away quickly.

"We haven't recovered the body yet," the officer continued. "With the rain swelling the creek we may not find it for a day or two." He lowered his voice and said, "I'm afraid we may have to ask you to come down again to identify it."

Meredith nodded. Seeing the dead boy's body with her own eyes would be a relief in a way. Then she would be sure his evil was banished forever. She trembled and leaned into Kit's arms.

But the body was never found.

Epilogue

Several days later and two hundred miles to the south, Shana Lewis paused before the floor-to-ceiling trophy case outside the administration office of Creighton Senior High School. Studying her reflection in the shiny glass, she smiled broadly in self-satisfaction, glad she had worked so hard to take off those extra five pounds. She didn't care if some of her teachers reprimanded her for wearing her short cheerleader's skirt to class — today was just too important. Besides, most of the student body — the male half in particular — wholeheartedly approved. That's who really mattered to her.

Shana smoothed her long blond hair away from her face and hurried upstairs to her locker. She wouldn't give the teachers anything to complain about if she could help it. She'd spend the day being as invisible as possible, saving everything she had for the final cheerleading competition after school. This was the competition she'd been waiting for, the competition she hoped would end with her being named captain of the senior squad. She had worked hard for three years for this moment — and she could hardly wait.

Shana turned into the hallway where her locker stood. She noticed a small box hanging on its handle.

Someone must be showering me with gifts already, she thought with a smile, and I haven't even won yet. I wonder what it could be.

She hurried forward, pulled the box off the locker and opened it. She gasped. Inside was a lock of blond hair and beneath the curl, written in blood-red letters were the words: YOU ARE IN MY POWER!